The Mermaid
By David Ralph

Text copyright © 2017 David Ralph Williams All Rights Reserved

This is a work of fiction. Names, characters, businesses, places, events and incidents are either the products of the author's imagination or used in a fictitious manner. Any resemblance to actual persons, living or dead, or actual events is purely coincidental.
David Ralph Williams 2017

I would like to dedicate this book to the following people.
This book is dedicated to my children, Luke, Hannah, Katie, of which Katie who found the original Mermaid's ring was instrumental in the inspiration for this story. This book is also dedicated to my wife Leesa, for putting up with all my little side projects over the years. This book is also dedicated to my parents, Hilda and Ralph for encouraging me to continue with my writing projects even though I had shelved this particular book for many years still incomplete. Special thanks to Solomon Barroa who kindly allowed me to use his wonderful artwork for the cover of this book.

Chapter 1
Journey to Siren's Dunes

Sophie had only five minutes to find what she was looking for. First she looked under her bed, then in it. She searched her cupboards and shelves and even inside her wardrobe. She had begun to fear that she had lost it somewhere and time was ticking away.

Sophie peeped out of her bedroom window. Her parents were waiting in the driveway by the car. Sophie's dad Tom kept on glancing at his watch and he shrugged his shoulders in a gesture at Sophie's mum, Helen, that made her go back into the house.

"Sophie love, it's getting late. We want to get a move on!" shouted Helen from the hallway. Sophie sighed. What was it her dad always said? 'When you lose something, try to retrace your actions. Think about the last place you used it.' Sophie thought hard.

"Sophie? We want to get going!" Helen continued to bellow from downstairs.

"Got it!" exclaimed Sophie, and she rushed over to her bedroom door. She unhooked her school bag from a wooden peg and delved inside. Sophie fished out her 3D dual screen gaming console. She remembered she had taken it to school for the last day of term. All the kids were allowed to bring a toy or game of their choice, and Sophie brought her favourite possession. Sophie hurriedly thrust her school bag back on its hook but knocked something else off a neighbouring hook. A well of emotion flooded through her as she picked up Kooler's lead.

Kooler was Sophie's dog. He was a border collie and she got him for her eighth birthday. She still remembered the day clearly and with fondness. Her dad came home from work a little later than usual. What she didn't know was that he'd driven to a local dog breeder and purchased Kooler for a surprise. When he eventually arrived home he was carrying a large brown box and he set it down on the kitchen floor. From out of that box toddled the most adorable puppy Sophie had ever seen.

Kooler was Sophie's best friend. He was the first person to greet her when she came in from school, and they did almost everything together. It was with some irony that close to her thirteenth birthday Kooler was taken away from her forever.

Sophie came home from school that day totally oblivious to the tragedy that awaited her. That day only four months ago was the first day in five years that Kooler was not waiting to greet her. Both her parents were upset when she walked into the lounge. Her mum was crying. Kooler had got out of the garden, through a loose plank in the fence. He had run out into the road and was hit by a lorry.

A vet had to put him down at the scene. Everyone was devastated and Sophie cried for days. Her dad said he would buy her another dog if she wished but Sophie refused. Kooler couldn't be replaced like that. Instead she would settle for just the memory of the best dog that ever was. Sophie's only regret apart from that terrible accident was that she never got to say goodbye to her best friend.

Sophie hung Kooler's lead back on its hook and she wiped her tears onto her sleeve.

"Sophie! If you can't find it just leave it. We have to go." It was her dad this time shouting.

"Coming Dad." Sophie slipped her games console into her travel bag and ran downstairs. Her dad was waiting for her in the hallway.

"At last. Did you find it?" Sophie nodded. Her eyes were red and puffy and Tom could see that she had been crying. He put his arm around her. "Don't be upset love, not today eh? It's the first day of our holidays."

"I know Dad, I just...just...you know," said Sophie not really explaining herself very well.

"I understand Sophie love but in a few hours we will be at Siren's dunes. It's a lovely place. Sun, sea, sand, and lots to do. You'll love it," Tom said blithely in an attempt to lighten the moment. Sophie smiled.

"Is there a fun fair?"

"A huge one," said Tom smiling.

"With a ghost train?"

"You bet," answered Tom still grinning.

"Then what are we waiting for?" They laughed together and left the house.

......

The drive from Cambridge to Siren's Dunes was a long one. Sophie had played with her games console for at least two hours before she grew tired of it. Helen and Sophie had played a spot of 'I spy' Sophie spied the white stripe in her mum's otherwise auburn locks, a trait they both shared. Tom made Sophie giggle when he referred to them as 'a couple of badgers'. Helen was not too amused with Tom's joke.

They stopped off at a service station that had a burger chain restaurant, and they ate lunch before continuing the last stretch of the journey. Sophie was given the task of spotting the first road sign for Siren's Dunes, if nothing else it kept her amused for a while. When she did finally catch sight of one she received the usual praise from Tom and Helen who acted as though they would never have found the place if it wasn't for her. Sophie accepted the praise dismissively because she knew her dad would have spent the whole of the previous night studying his road maps. He usually did.

They had booked a holiday cottage right in the centre of the old-world coastal town. Helen and Tom spoke about how beautiful it looked as Tom parked their car. The cottage was detached and was painted white with blue window frames. The house had a small country-cottage garden filled with lupins and rose bushes, and a collection of little statuettes of seagulls and elves. Sophie was first out of the car and she ran up to the little blue front gate. There was a plaque on it. '*Gull Cottage*' it read, and over the gate was a rose arch with golden roses entwined about it.

"Can I go in Mum?" asked Sophie holding onto the gate. She wanted to see inside the cottage and hoped it was similarly charming inside.

"Sure, catch!" Tom threw Sophie a bunch of keys; she caught them awkwardly.

"Oops!"

"It's the long brassy coloured one I think," said Tom. Sophie ran up the higgledy-piggledy path to the front door.

The inside of the house was as alluring as the outside. All of the rooms were small yet cosy. The ceiling of the lounge was covered with robust exposed beams and there was a lovely old wood burning stove set into the chimney breast. It was a shame the weather was warm; Sophie would have liked to see her dad build a nice fire. There was a little kitchen full of curious and attractive old-world cooking things, many of which were hanging from wooden racks attached to the ceiling. Sophie couldn't wait to see the bedrooms.

The master bedroom contained the largest bed Sophie had ever seen. It was a four poster with a top that almost reached the ceiling. Tom and Helen were delighted with it.

"It's a bed fit for a king," said Tom and he fell back onto it spreading out his arms. Sophie laughed

"Which room is mine?" Sophie asked.

"It's a three-bedroom house, so I guess you have a choice of two!" Helen replied.

"Wicked! I'll go and see," shouted Sophie and she dashed out of her parent's room and along the landing to the next door.

The first room had two twin beds with a table either side. There was an imposing oil painting hanging between both beds. The subject of the painting, was a rather elderly man with a long grey beard. His eyes were a funny colour, almost purple. The picture gave Sophie the creeps so she decided to use the other room.

The next bedroom was just perfect. A single large bed was set next to a small, crooked window. The view from the little window was lovely, you could see all the way down the sloping high street, right to the bottom where it appeared to merge with the ocean. There were no creepy pictures in this room though, instead there was a nice square mirror with a gold frame and lots of nice little drawers and cupboards. Tom and Helen came into the room.

"You like this one then?" asked Tom.

"Yeah, the other one has this awful spooky picture, but this room has a wicked view look!" Tom and Helen peered out of the little window.

"Yes you're right. You can see almost the whole town from here," said Helen.

"I thought we could leave unpacking till later, it's almost tea time. Let's have a quick look around the town then grab some nosh eh?" said Tom, he was feeling hungry. They all agreed and just left the bags and suitcase from the car in the hallway of the cottage. Helen and Sophie both changed their shoes for some comfortable trainers before they embarked on their amble through the town.

Chapter 2
Treasure in the sand

The high street sloped downwards to meet the sea front. Either side of the single cobbled street were rows of little shops and cafés. The buildings were a mismatch of old and new some of which bore signs informing the onlooker of their age. Tom was pleased to find a crooked Tudor style pub about halfway down the street, it was painted pink and black and the sign swinging in the sea breeze carried its name.

"The Mermaid," read Sophie out loud. The sign depicted a somewhat weather worn painting of such a fantastic creature.

"Yes, I'd like to pop in there," laughed Tom.

"Well you can't, not today anyway," rebuked Helen.

"I know love I was just kidding." Tom was slightly disappointed. They eventually came to the end of the street and discovered the promenade.

The sea front was a glitzy stretch of amusement arcades, dazzling white hotels, and fast food stalls. All of these were built upon a series of large and craggy cliffs, and Siren's Dunes even had its own lighthouse. The customary variety of maritime shops each sporting a full range of fishing nets, diving helmets, and plastic crabs were everywhere. Sophie spotted the funfair.

"Oh Mum, Dad, can we go to the fair pleeease!" she pleaded.

"I think it might be closing love." Helen could see a few of the rides had tarpaulin covers on. The three made their way over to the funfair regardless. Helen was right, there was a large white sign on a fence at the entrance stating clearly that the funfair shuts at five in the evening. Sophie was a little down hearted, nevertheless she examined the fair through the fence.

There were a huge variety of interesting and fun things contained within the boundaries of this park. In particular, Sophie noticed the large roller coaster called the *'Sea-Dragon'*, and next to this was a ghost train. In the middle of the park was a curious white cubicle constructed from aluminium double glazed windows and a door. A sign next to it read *'Izabela, World famous fortune teller.* Sophie wondered if there was such a person inside but all the windows were covered with laced drapes. Sophie also noticed a fun house and her most favourite ride of all, the Waltzers.

"Not to worry Sophie, we can come to the fair tomorrow, it's been a while since the three of us took a spin in the Waltzers," said Tom.

"It's okay. Can we walk on the sand?" Sophie asked, she could suddenly smell that salty sea air and was eager to see the deep blue sheets and famous golden sands of Siren's Dunes.

"Yes the sea air will give us an appetite, but I wonder if the tide is in?" Pondered Helen.

......

The tide wasn't in and they all descended some concrete steps from the promenade down to the sand. The sand was a beautiful colour, not like anything Sophie had ever seen before. She ran along the beach for a while in front of her parents. Tom and Helen held hands as they walked along, discussing the birds that were nesting in some nearby cliff walls. The sea looked marvellous at this time of the day, the sunlight glimmered off the surface in an almost magical way, it was so bright Sophie wished she had brought her sunglasses with her. Tom and Helen caught up with Sophie.

"Watch this," shouted Tom and he cast a stone onto the sea and they watched it skip the waves five or six times.

"Gosh! How do you do that?" asked Sophie impressed by her Father's trick.

"Well you have to find the right kind of stone for a start, a nice flat one." Sophie and her father began to hunt for such a pebble. After a multitude of failed attempts at skipping the waves with various stones, Sophie resorted to what she always did on the beach, she hunted for treasure.

The kind of treasure Sophie sought could be anything. An unusual stone, a beautiful shell or even a piece of curious driftwood. She would take her treasure home with her and it usually ended up in a small shell covered box that sat on her bookshelf. Sophie had plenty of such treasures discovered over the years, but nothing nearly as precious, nearly as fantastic as what she was about to discover this day. Tucked away, undisturbed, in the bright resplendent sand something twinkled at her.

Sophie plucked the object from out of the sand, she wiped it with her fingertips to remove the residual sand grains still clinging to it. It looked like a ring, opaque and green in colour, almost bottle green. Set in the face of the ring was what appeared to be a silvery pearl around which was engraved some unfathomable writing. Sophie clasped a tight hand around the object and rushed on to show it to her parents.

"Mum, Dad. Wait! I've found something," she shouted in between gulps of air. Tom and Helen paused in there dawdle.

"What have you found love?" asked Helen amused at Sophie's sudden serious face.

"Treasure, real treasure!" Sophie opened her hand to reveal the ring sitting on her palm. Tom picked it up and examined it.

"Hmm. It's unusual, yes very unusual," Tom said. Helen snatched it off him.

"Let me see it. Oh, it's just a piece of sea glass, that's all." Helen dismissed the idea that it could be anything really unusual.

"Oh come on now. How can it be sea glass? It's a perfect band look," said Tom adamant his daughter had indeed found something exotic. Helen turned it around in her fingers.

"It's a bottle, you know, the neck, or the rim of the spout! The waves have polished and smoothed it over, that's all." Sophie took the ring back from her mother. Whatever it was, bottle neck or ring, she was keeping it.

Another half mile along the sand and the three climbed back up to the promenade using some more concrete steps. These steps had an old rusty rail attached to them, Tom pointed them out telling Helen and Sophie that it was the salt that corrodes the iron. Back on the promenade they were lucky to be close to Neptune's Fish Bar.

"Well the sea air has given me an appetite! What about you two?" Tom asked. Both Helen and Sophie nodded in agreement and they all slipped into Neptune's café for a slap up feed of cod and chips.

Chapter 3
A maiden o' the sea

Back at the holiday cottage it was twilight. Tom was reading a book in an armchair. The book was a local history of Siren's dunes. He was searching for interesting places to visit during the week. Sophie was just finishing a banana milk shake her mother had made her. She was wearing her pyjamas as it was almost time for bed.

"We will be rising early tomorrow because we have lots to do," said Helen as she took Sophie's empty glass from her.

"I know Mum, goodnight. Goodnight Dad," Sophie said and she climbed the stairs to bed.

"Goodnight Sophie," Tom shouted from his armchair, "and don't forget to clean your teeth!" he added.

After scrubbing her teeth in the bathroom Sophie walked across the landing passing the bedroom with the spooky portrait. She closed the door to that room and slipped into the room that she found friendlier.

Sophie had brought a book with her to read in bed during her holiday. The book was about a boy wizard and his friends. The boy enjoyed many fantastic adventures and Sophie wished her life could be as exiting. She marked a page with a dog-ear because the reading had made her sleepy. Sophie was about to close her eyes and settle down in her comfy bunk when she remembered something important. Reaching over to a bundle of discarded clothes, Sophie rooted about in one of the pockets of her jeans. She fished out the treasure she had found on the beach that very afternoon, her sea ring.

Sophie turned the green band over in her fingers. Even though its texture was frosted she noticed how it caught the glow from her little bedside lamp and sparkled beautifully. The centre orb or pearl for a moment seemed to flash back at her as though it were a tiny bulb. Sophie noticed the etched writing again around the pearl. It was very small and she could barely make it out. She wished she had brought a magnifying glass with her, and she strained her eyes to read the word. 'Melusa' she thought it said. She wasn't sure as the writing was joined up and looked sort of old fashioned. Was Melusa a place? She thought it sounded like a name. Sophie wondered.

Sophie continued to gaze at the ring until she could barely stay awake. She slipped the ring onto the middle finger of her left hand so that it would not get lost in the bed sheets, and then she closed her eyes. In seconds Sophie fell into a deep sleep.

......

Sophie dreamed an unusual dream. She was in a cavern. Beautifully coloured stalactites hung from the ceiling. The cavern was filled with boxes of fabulous jewels, gold, and other valuable trinkets. She was aware that she was sitting on a rock and looking at the centre of the cavern floor. There was a rippling pool of dazzling water. The water looked lovely and inviting, and Sophie plunged in.

Now underwater, Sophie was aware of the coldness and the darkness around her. She followed a school of silvery fish towards a distant blanket of light above her. As she propelled herself nearer to the light she realised that it was the surface of the water with the sun's rays cutting through from above sending down shafts of sunlight. The sun felt warm on her face as she broke the surface.

In the dream Sophie now bobbed about on the surface of a calm sea. Even though her underwater swim had been a long one, she did not find herself gulping for air, the need was not there at all. Sophie took in her surroundings. She could make out the shoreline, and guessed that she was about half a mile out at sea. She didn't feel fear at finding herself alone on the sea. In fact, it felt natural to her, not scary at all. What land she could see looked like Siren's Dunes but many things were missing. The cliffs were there, although they looked higher, more impressive than when she was walking on the beach earlier. The lighthouse was visible, but all the hotels and amusements were missing. She couldn't even see the funfair.

Sophie became aware of something creaking and sloshing behind her. Twisting her body in the water she turned and saw a sailing ship, gliding effortlessly past her. The ship's sails were inflated and its crew were busy hauling in vast fishing nets. Sophie felt something pulling at her submerged body, dragging her down into the water. She became scared and thought some monstrous shark had her feet in its jaws. Sophie was wrong.

When her head went under the surface, she could see she had become tangled in another large fishing net. Sophie struggled to free herself but the harder she struggled and wriggled, the more tangled up she became. One of her arms had got caught between knots of the netting. As she yanked her arm free, a large knot knocked off the sea ring from her finger. Sophie watched the ring sink into the dark depths, in seconds it was out of sight, lost to the seabed floor. Soon the net was being dragged out of the sea. Sophie was upside-down and still caught up in the fishing net. Her body hit the barnacle-encrusted planks of the ship's bow and it hurt. Sophie became frightened. She couldn't see her legs, only this huge fishy tail which flapped each time she tried to move them. The two crewmen who had been tugging in the huge net suddenly stopped and pointed at her.

"Bless me socks!" said one of the crewmen, "we have caught us ere a maiden o' the sea lad."

"Throw it back, it be cursed, we all be cursed," wailed the other. Sophie could only think about her ring and how she would ever find it now. The crewmen let go of the net and Sophie was cast into the cool dark waters once more. Down and down she sank, still struggling in the netting. Down and down, and darker and darker.

Sophie sat up in her bed. She gulped for air but she had no idea why she was doing it. Sophie realised that she'd been having a nightmare, she quickly tried hard to remember it, but like always she couldn't. She felt for her hand and checked to see if she could feel the sea ring on her finger. She could. Sophie snuggled up in bed once more and closed her eyes. Oh, if only she could remember the dream she thought, and then drifted to sleep once more.

Chapter 4
Afraid in the ghost train

They were spinning around so fast now, and Sophie had to hold onto the metal bar to stop herself sliding about on the seat. The Waltzers had always been her favourite ride and the first one she ran to the moment they had entered the funfair. Tom was roaring a series of 'Yeehaas' every time the carriage twirled around. Helen was watching them both from the safety of the side lines. She didn't particularly like this ride as it made her feel queasy. Helen took a photo of Tom and Sophie as they spun past, she was using Sophie's old Polaroid camera.

The carriage eventually slowed down to a complete stop and Tom helped Sophie out.

"Gosh! I love that ride Dad." Sophie could hardly walk in a straight line.

"My head's still spinning, my brain's doing laps," laughed Tom. Helen greeted the giggling pair

"Right, what's next? The roller coaster?" Helen teased.

"Oh no way Mum! Not just yet anyways. I feel kinda sick. But that was wicked! Right Dad?"

"You bet. What about the ghost train?" Tom pointed over to the foreboding display ahead of them. It was painted to look like a haunted castle, with battlements and turrets. There were life size models of werewolves, vampires, and mummies at various positions around the ticket booth.

"Cool! Let's go on it Dad." Sophie ran over to the ride and joined the queue.

There were about four other people waiting at the ticket booth behind Sophie. Helen declined a ride on the ghost train saying she had to look after the coats and bags. Tom joined Sophie and they waited for the train to emerge from within the castle.

Two large wooden doors were bashed open by a long set of carriages that resembled a monstrous snake. The carriages were filled with people, some were laughing and some still had their eyes firmly shut. A man from the ticket booth lifted bars on the sides of all the carriages and the occupants clambered out and made their way out of the turnstile at the other side of the booth. Tom paid the ticket man five pounds.

"Sophie go and choose a carriage love." Tom said waiting for his change. Sophie knew exactly what carriage to choose. As she was first in the queue it was her privilege to take the front carriage, the head of the snake. Tom joined her squeezing into the green reptilian textured carriage.

Whilst waiting for the ride to start, Sophie waved at her mother who smiled back at her. Helen wanted to take another photo and Tom joked pulling a frightened face. They both felt a jolt as the train sprung to life. The huge green snake head smashed through two swinging doors that had a notice painted onto them. The notice read, 'AT ALL TIMES KEEP YOUR LEGS AND ARMS INSIDE THE TRAIN. DO NOT GET OUT OF

THE TRAIN'. Sophie squeezed up next to Tom as they were suddenly plunged into darkness.

A laughing skull illuminated the first dark corridor. A vampire bat flew into view. Two ghastly devils danced and tried to grab at them. A cobweb brushed Sophie's face. A glowing pumpkin stared with evil eyes. A skeleton was riding a bike. Sophie huddled close to her dad as the noises became louder and the whole ride became darker. A blast of air shot down from above and something lit up ahead of them both. There were cries and screams coming from the back of the train. Sophie felt afraid when she looked at the vision in front. An enormous mermaid, glowing eerily barred their path. This mermaid did not look like it came from out of a Disney cartoon. Its hair was wild and green, and its face was a snarling wicked mask. Sophie gripped Tom's arm tightly

"Easy love, that hurts!" Sophie remembered something. Something from a dream. She felt cold as a draught of air flowed past their carriage. The sea was cold she thought. Sophie closed her eyes tight as the train crashed through the mermaid.

The daylight was so bright in contrast to the darkness inside the ghost train. Sophie still had her eyes closed when the man from the ticket booth lifted the restraining bars on the carriages.

"Come on Sophie," Tom saw that Sophie had screwed up her eyes and wasn't budging a bit. "The ride's over love, time to get off now." Sophie opened her eyes. It took a moment or two for her eyes to adjust to the strong sunshine. Everything looked kind of pale for a moment and then the colours started to flood back and fill everything up. She was clutching her sea ring.

"Sorry Dad, I. . . I was a bit scared!"

"Scared? Of the ghost train? That's unlike you love."

"I know. It was the woman. . . the mermaid. . . I think!"

Helen joined Tom and Sophie at the exit gate. Sophie regained her composure and shrugged off the fear that had overcome her moments before. She didn't want her mum to know that she had been afraid in case she started becoming over protective again. After Kooler died, Sophie had had some bad dreams. She thought that was all over now.

"Right you two monsters. Let's get something nice to eat. Candyfloss or ice cream?"

"Candyfloss for me Mum!"

"I don't know, I think I feel like a doughnut," Tom said as he caught a whiff of a nearby stall selling the sweetened fried cakes.

Sophie, Helen, and Tom all purchased what they wanted and decided to walk along whilst they ate, taking in the rest of the fair. Sophie kept on thinking about the mermaid as she licked at her fluffy mass of spun sugar. She wondered what it all meant. The fear of the mermaid, and the fragments of a dream that floated about inside her head like unmanned ships. Tom threw his empty doughnut bag into a litter bin and then brushed his hands together to remove the sugar that clung to his fingers.

"Helen love, you haven't had a go on anything yet."

"I know, but you know I don't like rides much. Besides, I am happy minding our stuff while you and Sophie enjoy yourselves."

"You have to go on something Mum," Sophie said adamant. Helen cast a glance in various directions, then something caught her eye.

"Okay then, I'd like to have my fortune read!" Helen pointed over to the square white cubicle ahead of them. It was a fortune teller's booth, and the sign outside read 'OPEN'.

"You must be joking! You don't believe in that do you?" laughed Tom. Helen ignored Tom's ridicule.

"You said I had to go on something, well, I want to have my fortune told."

"Okay love, if it makes you happy." They all made their way over to 'Izabela's' booth. As they drew near, Sophie thought she saw the lace curtains that covered every window on the booth twitching as though someone was peering out at them.

Chapter 5
Izabela's booth

The door to the booth was open and a long curtain covering the entrance fluttered in the breeze.

"Well, what are you waiting for?" asked Tom. Helen seemed reluctant to go inside.

"I. . . I thought there might be a sign, you know with a price on it. I wondered how much it cost." Before Helen could say anymore the curtain covering the entrance was parted and out stepped a curious looking woman.

The woman was little, about four feet ten inches roughly. She wore a scarlet scarf on her head that she had wrapped around and tied in a peculiar manner. She wore a white blouse that was all flappy and loose, and a long black skirt trailed to the floor obscuring her feet. The woman was about forty years old and had raven black hair visible below her scarf. Her face was quite pleasant though and she was smiling at them.

"I bid you welcome. Is there anything I can do for you here today? Anything you wish to know?" The woman spoke in an unusual accent, foreign, but Sophie couldn't decide where she was from.

"Erm. . . yes! We. . . I mean, I would like my fortune read, if it's okay I mean," said Helen awkwardly. The little woman looked Helen over briefly.

"Why of course it is okay. Reading fortunes is what I do. And, I am very good you know!" she pointed at her sign above the front window of the booth, "Izabela, world famous fortune teller," she read. "Please come inside, all of you." They all followed Izabela into her booth.

Outside the booth a tall skinny man was pushing a wheeled rubbish cart. The man stopped near the booth and used a long stick with a sharp point on the end to pick up some discarded sweet wrappers and chip papers. He put the rubbish into a bin on his cart then he stopped for a rest, leaning on the corner of the booth. The man took a small silver flask from out of his trouser pocket and he unscrewed the top. He took a swig from the flask and coughed.

"Blimey, that's rough that is!" he spluttered out loud. It was a warm morning. Nobody would mind if he stopped for a rest. His feet were killing him, and besides, he was thinking of giving this job up for good. "Old Jack can do better than this, better than picking up other people's rubbish," he thought out loud. Rubbing a silvery bristled chin, Jack continued to indulge himself from his flask.

......

The inside of Izabela's booth was fascinating to Sophie. There was a little round table in the middle of the booth upon which sat the most beautiful thing she had ever seen. A huge round crystal ball sparkled from the light of six small flickering candles neatly placed around the booth.

There were pictures of strange scenes from far off lands, one of them showed a radiant tree with people dancing about its trunk. There were also lots of wooden boxes and odd figurines arranged upon a small sideboard. Sophie sat on a small wicker chair near to the door and Tom sat beside her. Helen was asked to sit at the central round table and Izabela joined her. Izabela reached over to one of the wooden boxes, she opened the lid and produced a thick stack of large cards. She handed the stack of cards to Helen.

"Oh look Tom, Fortune cards!" shouted Helen in excitement.

"Please, would you shuffle the Tarot deck," Izabela requested. Helen did her best to shuffle the cards but they were large and her shuffling was a bit clumsy. Helen handed the cards back to Izabela.

"Sometimes I look into my crystal ball. Sometimes I use the cards. I think the cards will be best today," said Izabela and she laid the cards out before her.

"Why would cards be best?" asked Helen. She was curious why the cards were chosen instead of the crystal ball.

"It depends upon the person. I have a feeling for such things. With you I feel that the cards will give you what you want."

"Oh, I see."

"I also perform psychometry. Do you know what that is?" Helen shook her head. "It means that I can take an object and hold it in my hand. I can then see pictures in my mind's eye of who the object belonged to. Feel their thoughts and feelings. But you are interested in the hereafter. These cards will give me a glimpse of the future, your future. But be warned, some people don't like what they hear." Izabela studied the cards and began to tell what she could see.

Tom and Sophie sat patiently whilst Helen listened to Izabela's predictions. Apparently, Helen was to receive some money from a relative. Tom got excited when there was mention of buying a larger house. Sophie was interested in hearing that she may soon have a little brother or sister, but she thought that her mum was probably too old for that now. There was mention of a foreign holiday and America in particular. Izabela also warned Helen to avoid eating seafood during this holiday, and to lock up the house securely. Helen wondered if she meant their holiday cottage or their real home in Cambridge. Izabela became concerned by one of her cards; she kept shaking her head and muttering to herself. Sophie sat up straight in her chair to try to get a good look at the particular card that Izabela seemed to be confused by. Sophie was unaware that she was fiddling with the sea ring as she watched Izabela. She was twisting the ring round and round her finger until it accidentally slipped of her finger and fell onto the floor of the fortune booth.

The sea ring rolled upon its edge underneath the table where Helen sat and came to rest next to Izabela's foot. The dropped ring broke Izabela's concentration and she looked straight at Sophie.

"Sorry," apologised Sophie. Izabela bent over to pick up the ring. She held it between her forefinger and thumb.

"Interesting," she said, but then she became rigid and her hand started to tremble.

"Are you alright?" Helen asked. She could see that Izabela had suddenly become affected by something. She feared that it may be some kind of seizure.

"This ring! How did you come by it?" asked Izabela in a serious tone.

"I... I found it, on the beach." Said Sophie.

"This ring belongs to someone very special. Do you know what it is?"

"No. I... I think it might be a bit of a bottle. My mum says it cou–" Izabela cut Sophie's reply short.

"This ring is no piece of bottle. It is the ring of a spirit. A spirit of the sea. A mermaid."

"A mermaid!" Sophie was fascinated by what Izabela had said, "a real mermaid?"

"Yes child. I told you I could read an object, see the pictures. A mermaid I saw. Our mermaid."

"Our mermaid?" What Izabela meant puzzled Sophie.

"The legends of mermaids are well known and believed by the folk of Siren's Dunes, it's how this place got its name. The sirens, or mermaids, were once common around these shores. There are many stories past down from local seafarers who had encountered them."

"Helen was beginning to doubt the sanity of the strange little woman who sat before her. She didn't like her filling Sophie's head with all kinds of nonsense.

"Well thank you very much. Your cards were very good but we must be on our way now. How much do I owe you?" Helen produced her purse and was waiting for Izabela to respond. Izabela did not take her eyes from Sophie.

"You must take this back to where you found it. If you don't it may be very unlucky for you!" Izabela touched the white stripe that spilled out from Sophie's otherwise dark curls, "Curious," she said.

"Excuse me. I asked how much I owed you." Helen said impatiently.

"Forgive me, I. . . I was distracted by your daughter's lovely trinket. Do not worry about the money, just make sure she takes the ring back."

"No charge? Are you sure?"

"Yes, I don't feel that I gave a good enough reading. Maybe if you came back another day?" said Izabela as she handed Sophie back her ring. Tom and Helen left Izabela's booth first followed then by Sophie who trailed behind. Izabela caught Sophie's arm to get her attention.

"Remember, take the ring back. Throw it into the sea. The mermaid will want it back. It is not for humans to have. It gives them power over her." Sophie didn't speak, she just nodded at Izabela who then released her grip on Sophie's arm.

"Come on love. We have. . . to. . . GO!" Tom shouted when he realised Sophie was still at the booth. Sophie scurried along to catch up with her parents. Izabela watched them go, she was concerned. She hoped that the girl would listen to

29

her. A young boy ran up to Izabela, it was Lon her son.

"Where have you been? Go on inside lad, I'll put the kettle on." Lon and Izabela disappeared inside the veiled booth.

Jack pushed his rubbish cart slowly along the path. He was following Sophie and her parents. Jack had heard everything Izabela, the 'Old Witch', as he referred to her by, had said to these people. He had listened in by the doorway of the booth. He was always nosey like that. But sometimes being nosey enlightened Jack to a crucial piece of information.

Like everyone else at Siren's Dunes, Jack had grown up listening to the tales and legends of the mermaids. Jack's father himself claimed to have spotted one whilst out on his fishing boat one dark and moonless night. Jack believed in such fantastical creatures. Unlike the other people of the town, he dreamed of having power over them, forcing them to do his bidding. Like a genie will serve its master. Jack thought that if he could get hold of that ring, the ring Izabela said belonged to a mermaid, he would become rich and powerful with such a creature as his servant.

Jack had heard the legends of subterranean caverns filled with diamonds and gold that the sirens had plundered from shipwrecks over the centuries. He wanted that treasure. With that ring, there would be no more need for the burglaries. No more risk of being caught by the police. For once he would get lucky, get rich. There would be an end to people pointing a finger at him, laughing at him, laughing at old Jack, the hopeless nobody, with his rubbish cart. Keeping his distance, Jack continued to keep a scheming eye on the family ahead of him.

Chapter 6
A dazzling display

The hut was very gloomy inside, but once Sophie had been in there for a few minutes her eyes adjusted and she could see an array of posters and photographs all pinned to the walls. The hut was a kind of local history centre for Siren's Dunes. There were maps of the town and old photographs taken during the Victorian days. The old photographs made Sophie chuckle, the people in the photographs wore very odd clothing as they bathed off shore. Helen popped her head around the door of the hut.

"Sophie, your dad is going to the café to buy a drink, what would you like?"

"Oh, a cola, no, lemonade please," answered Sophie. Helen disappeared outside and left Sophie alone again.

The hut was positioned on a grassy cliff top near to the town light house. There was a little café opposite and some tables and chairs set out on a patio. Helen and Tom wanted to have a rest before they explored more of the town. Sophie had been interested in looking inside the hut as soon as she saw it. It was quite old, probably Victorian. It stood robust and proud upon the cliff top. It was painted white and blue so many times over the years that it had lost its sharp edges and corners giving it a softer, rounded appearance.

The hut and café area was quite deserted with only Sophie and her parents taking refreshment.

Sophie was glad at the lack of others to disturb her interesting look back through time. Along with the old photographs there were newspaper articles pinned to the walls, most of them had headlines telling of local disasters. In 1984 apparently, there was a large fire along the sea front which destroyed three of the larger hotels. More recently there had been some local flooding, and one newspaper showed a man in a dinghy paddling himself along the main street which leads up to where their holiday cottage was situated. But it was what was pinned to the right of the newspaper articles that caught Sophie's attention.

A collection of colourful mermaids all drawn by pupils of Sandy Grange Juniors were displayed for visitors to see. The pictures were all hung under the heading, 'OUR MERMAID'. Sophie studied each and every picture and began fiddling with her sea ring again. She remembered the mermaid painted in the ghost train and how it frightened her. Sophie almost recalled a fragment from her nightmare but it slipped out of her mind so quickly again and was lost. Sophie looked at the sea ring that felt almost warm wrapped around her finger.

Izabela had told her to take the ring back to the beach, but it was so beautiful, so special. She didn't want to part with it. If it really was a mermaid's ring, then it would be the best thing she had ever found, ever owned. Sophie saw a large poster that was placed beneath the array of Sandy Grange's colourful mermaids. The poster contained recorded sightings of mermaids from fishermen, women, and children within the local community of Siren's Dunes. Sophie read two of the sightings.

'Off the shore of Siren's Dunes, 1783, six fishermen affirmed that they had found a mermaid entangled in their herring drift-net. On examining their captive, she was found to be four feet long with stiff bristles on the top of her head extending down to her shoulder, like a crest. She had neither gills or scales on her upper body. The mermaid had a beautiful complexion and could not be more lovely or exactly formed in all parts above the waist resembling a complete young woman. Below the waist she was all fish with fins and a huge spreading tail. The fishermen who were very superstitious cast their nets back into the sea. The mermaid wriggled free from the nets and dived down in a perpendicular direction'

'1947, an eighty-year-old fisherman reported seeing a mermaid in the sea roughly thirty yards from shore, lying on top of a floating lobster box combing her hair. As soon as the mermaid realised she had been seen she dived back into the sea. Nobody at Siren's Dunes could break the fisherman's firm conviction that he had seen a mermaid'

The ring on Sophie's finger became so hot she had to slip it off for a moment. She rubbed the skin on her finger and left the hut. Sophie joined Tom and Helen as they sat on the patio chairs at the little café opposite the hut. Tom was drinking a mug of tea and Helen was drinking water from a bottle.

"What are we doing next Mum?" Sophie enquired.

"Well we thought we would have another little look around the shops, buy something for your nan and granddad, then maybe go someplace for dinner."

"Can we go on the beach again?"

"Of course, if you want to."

Sophie was eager to return to the beach. Maybe she would do what Izabela had told her to do, leave the ring on the sand, where she had found it. Maybe she wouldn't. Whatever the decision, Sophie felt somehow drawn to the beach, to the sea but she had no idea why.

"Finished?" asked Tom pointing to Sophie's drink. Sophie gulped down the last few drops of her lemonade and they all left the café. A cool breeze had begun to creep in from the sea and it lifted Sophie's discarded can of lemonade from out of the top of a heavily filled rubbish basket. The can was pushed along the café patio by the winds invisible playful fingers until it came to rest by a worn, old boot. The boot covered a foot, old Jack's foot. Jack bent down to pick up the can then tossed it back into the rubbish bin, "old habits die hard," he chuckled to himself. Keeping Sophie, Helen and Tom firmly in his sights Jack dawdled along some distance behind.

......

It was almost seven in the evening. Sophie had just enjoyed a pizza dinner with her parents and now they were all back on the sand. The tide was slowly rolling in and Sophie played a game with the waves, walking boldly towards the receding foamy waters then leaping backwards before a new incoming breaker soaked her feet. Sophie enjoyed this game a lot. It helped take her mind off the decision she was trying to make. Should she drop the mermaid's ring on the sand and walk away? Or should she keep the ring?

Helen and Tom sat down together on Tom's coat. He had been carrying it all day in case it rained. The weather was too warm to wear it, but it made a handy beach blanket. Tom and Helen watched Sophie as she explored the various rock pools that were scattered about. Sophie always enjoyed investigating rock pools. They were little wildlife habitats cut off temporarily from the mother sea. She would mostly seek crabs that would hide underneath rocks or clumps of seaweed. Sometimes small shrimps could be found. The rock pool Sophie was preoccupied with contained an unusual white crab.

Sophie had learnt how to pick up a crab without it nipping her with its claw. She carefully dunked her hand into the cool salty water. Before she could even touch the crab's shell she gasped in amazement. The mermaid's ring still on her index finger submerged within the rock pool began to glow. Sophie quickly retracted her hand and brought her hand nearer her face so she could get a good look at the ring. It didn't appear half as fluorescent as it did whilst under water, however it was glowing faintly. It was like one of those glow-in-the-dark toys you hold underneath a light bulb, when the light is switched off the toy shines with an eerie green light. But those toys only worked in the dark unlike the ring which was shining brightly even in the daylight. Sophie dunked her hand back into the rock pool.

This time she held her hand submerged for much longer, examining the ring. The green light that the ring emitted was so intense that it illuminated the entire rock pool. The rippling light was reflected back onto Sophie's face. The central orb on the ring began to pulse with a strong white light. Sophie began to hear a sound, distant at first but steadily growing stronger, louder. It was difficult for her to tell whether the sound was inside her head or actually in the real world. It sounded like a voice, singing. The singing was in the real world and somebody else could hear it too. Old Jack was watching Sophie from above on the promenade. He saw the ring's dazzling display in the rock pool.

"Well I'll be!" Jack blurted to himself. The old witch was right he thought. That ring is a magical ring. And as soon as it was in his possession, the better off he'd be. Jack crouched low down and pretended to tie his boot lace. He could see Sophie's parents were now on their feet and walking over to where she was. He didn't want anybody to see him there.

Tom and Helen had almost caught up with Sophie when the ring finally lost its sparkle. Sophie had had the ring out of the water for a couple of minutes now and it seemed to have returned to normal although it felt warm to the touch.

"Sophie, was that you singing?" asked Tom.

"Nope."

"Are you sure? We could have sworn we heard singing, sort of weird singing really!"

"No Dad, I think it might have come from the fairground, you know."

"Perhaps you're right. Find anything interesting?"

"Hmm, not really. Just an old crab." Sophie hated lying to her parents but they would never believe what she had just seen the ring do, never understand. She hardly understood herself.

"Come on then, we're going back to the cottage, that's enough for one day." Helen said and she led the way back towards the rusty rail and steps that climbed up to the promenade. Sophie slipped the ring off her finger and held it in the palm of her other hand. She waited for Tom to walk ahead of her. It was now or never, she told herself. Would she drop the ring and walk away? Or would she keep it?

For a moment Sophie thought about Izabela and what she had just seen the ring do. Maybe she was frightened of it now. Perhaps the power that came from it might do her harm. Sophie held the ring out over the rock pool, she almost let it go, part of her wanted rid of it. But at the last moment she closed her hand around it and caught up with her parents.

Jack had seen Sophie holding the ring over the pool, looking as though she was about to let it drop. At that moment he hoped she would. It would be a lot easier for him if she had. But the silly girl had put it back in her pocket. Now he would have the risky business of taking it from her himself. Jack took a swig from his little flask then popped it back in his pocket. He'll get that ring he thought. One way or another.

Chapter 7
Old houses have voices

Bedtime at the holiday cottage was always preceded by a game. Tonight they were all playing a game of cards. Sophie had bought the playing cards herself whilst they were all out shopping. The backs of the deck showed a picture of Siren's Dunes during night with the town illuminated by strings of coloured bulbs hanging from the street lamps. Also on the picture was the lighthouse sending its warning beams out across the sea.

They were playing a game Tom called happy families, where you had to collect two sets of four of a kind. The winner is the one who completes their sets first. Sophie was only waiting for one more king to complete her second set, she already had four sevens and it was her turn to take a card.

"Yehaa! I'm the winner!" Sophie shouted as she turned over the card to reveal the king of diamonds. She placed both her sets of cards down on the carpet to reveal her claim to victory.

"Well I can't argue with that, you beat us again," said Tom.

"One more game, you might win next time."

"It will have to wait until tomorrow, its eleven o'clock and past your bedtime," added Helen.

"Oh Mum!"

"Never mind oh Mum! Come on let's have you upstairs." Sophie put her cards away in their little box and finished her drink of milkshake. She bid her parents goodnight and climbed the stairs to bed. Tom cleared away empty glasses and some saucers from the cake they had shared earlier in the evening.

"This holiday seems to have helped Sophie get over Kooler," Tom said as he carried the crockery into the kitchen.

"Yes, she has brightened up. Everyone enjoys a holiday Tom, even me!"

"It is nice here isn't it, a real old fashioned seaside town."

"Well it suits us then, because we are sort of old fashioned people."

"Yes we are dear. Shall we retire madam, to the bed chamber?" Tom laughed as he turned off the lights to the lower house. Soon everyone was in bed and the house fell silent.

......

Jack had been watching the cottage from an old bench on the street opposite. He had waited for almost four hours without moving an inch. When the lights to the downstairs finally went off he started to fidget. He was always nervous about breaking into a house even though he had been doing it most of his life. In fact, he had burgled this cottage many times over the years, as it was unoccupied sometimes for weeks on end.

It was ten past midnight. Jack guessed that everyone would be asleep by now. He crept around the back of the cottage and stood before a little window that looked into the kitchen. This window had a very old fashioned latch and Jack knew just how to pop it open. Jack eased himself into the kitchen using the heavy old sink and draining board as a support. Now he was in the cottage. He produced a little torch from a pocket and turned it on. The beam was weak and he cursed himself for forgetting to buy some new batteries. The torch did provide some illumination. It was enough for Jack to find the stairs and to stealthily scale them.

The cottage was old, and old houses have voices. Many of the stairs would creak and snap like an angry cat the moment you put your weight onto them. Jack knew by memory which were the worst and he avoided them cleverly. Soon Jack had reached the landing and three doors confronted him. He opened the first door. It led to the master room. Tom and Helen were fast asleep. Tom was snoring and snorting like a hog. Jack was about to close the door and look for Sophie's room when something caught his eye. To Jack's right there was a little set of drawers, and on top was Helen's jewellery box. He scooped up the box and closed the door tightly.

The second door was opened to reveal an unoccupied room. Jack peered inside the gloomy interior and the familiar sight of the bearded old man in the painting greeted him. He saluted the painting. It was a kind of superstition for Jack. For as long as he could remember, that painting had been in the cottage, and the face of that old man always seemed to be judging him.

The third and final door could only lead Jack to the mermaid's ring, and he was right. Sophie was curled up fast asleep in her bed. Jack shone his torch into the room and its beam glided up and over the various cupboards and shelves like some ghostly orb. Soon he had discovered the whereabouts of the ring. His beam picked out the glossy band as it echoed the torch's rays back at him.

"Ahh," whispered Jack to himself. He carefully crept over to the side of Sophie's bed. The ring was perched on top of a thick novel which Sophie had been reading that night. He switched off his torch and picked up the ring.

"Jesus wept!" shrieked Jack, the ring felt red hot as though made of molten metal. He dropped the ring and his torch then sucked his fingers. Sophie stirred in her sleep and Jack cursed himself for making such an outburst. Jack waited for Sophie to fall still once more and he took a handkerchief from his pocket and gathered up the ring from the floor. It felt cold now and a puzzled Jack slipped it into his trouser pocket.

Jack was delighted at his success and he made his way back down the stairs and to the open kitchen window. Before he left he took out his little flask and gulped down the last few drops of whatever noxious brew he kept in it. With his nerves now steady, Jack climbed back out through the window and jogged away from the cottage and down the high street towards the promenade.

Chapter 8
An ancient signal

Jack felt like a little child with a new toy. Except the ring was no toy. It was a fabled treasure that had the power to make him rich, and Jack couldn't wait. He leapt down the steps that led off the promenade and onto the beach, and he ran along the sands towards an outcrop of sea sprayed rocks.

Jack climbed on top of the largest boulder, the waves crashed against it sending up salty spray that threatened to soak him. Jack didn't care about getting wet, he lay on his stomach and produced the ring from his pocket. Jack tried to push the ring onto one of his fingers but his fingers were too podgy, instead Jack held the ring between his forefinger and thumb and dangled it into the choppy water. Immediately the ring sparkled into life. A brilliant green light emanated from it and the central orb pulsed an ancient signal down into the depths. Jack lay for quite a while with his hand submerged, his shoulder was going stiff and he almost withdrew his arm, but then the sound started.

It was the same sound he had heard earlier that day when Sophie had the ring dipped into the rock pool. It was a soothing, yet haunting singing and it was coming from far out at sea. Jack's arm was turning blue with the cold and a horrible numbness was creeping up his shoulder. Just when he thought he could bear it no longer the singing stopped. Jack lifted his arm out of the water. The ring was dull once more.

"Eh? No, it can't be!" Jack stood up and balanced himself unsteadily on the slippery rock. He whacked the ring against the rock in frustration. "Just a stupid novelty, that's all. A stupid kids toy!" He roared. Jack was about to cast the ring into the sea when he saw something.

There was something on the surface of the sea, picked out by a full moon's light. It was about forty feet off shore and heading towards the outcrop of rocks, towards Jack. He strained his eyes to try to make out what it could be. He thought it might be a seal, or even a lump of driftwood but it was hard to tell. The thing was only about twenty feet away from him now and it appeared to duck down into the water.

Jack studied the surface of the water where he had last seen the thing. But there was nothing to be seen, only swirling clods of seaweed. *SPLASH.* Something broke the surface of the water near to the side of Jack's rock. The noise frightened him and he slipped on the rock, landing on his arse. Jack sat up and rubbed his back. He was aware of somebody moving about the rocks, in the water.

"Eh? Who are ye? What you want?" Jack said feeling a little dazed. He reached into his pocket looking for his little torch but it wasn't there.

"Are you the one who holds the ring, and has the power to make it sing?" a beautiful voice sang out. Jack stood up unsteadily and looked about him.

"Aye, I got the ring see!" Jack saw a darkened shadow, a person, bobbing about on the surface of the water. Jack edged closer to the end of the rock to get a good look. He was amazed by what he saw. A woman, glided gracefully through the water towards his rock. As she came nearer, the moonlight made her features visible to Jack.

She had a beautiful yet exotic face. Her eyes were yellow and shone like gold. Her hair, a mixture of thick red and green strands looked like seaweed and it floated on the surface of the water about her. Her skin looked normal yet pale and it had a kind of sparkle as though it had been dusted with tiny specs of glitter. Her mouth although perfectly formed seemed larger than it should be and she opened and closed her mouth as if imitating a fish.

"Ooh! You be the mermaid you are!" Jack spluttered. His wide eyes looked her over.

"Melusa is my name, for you I came."

"And this be your ring?" Jack held up the ring to show the strange woman who floated before him.

"Who holds my ring and calls to me, from my home beneath the sea?"

"I am Jack, I. . . I be your master now. You must do as I say whilst I have this see!" Jack saw the mermaid's face change from a placid smile to an unpleasant scowl. Her eyes shone brighter and Jack became scared fearing some powerful bolts of lightning would explode from them and frazzle him where he stood. The thunder and fury melted from her face and was replaced with an expression of sorrow.

"I want. . . want to be rich! You can make me rich eh?" Jack sneered.

"Your heart is black and full of greed, you humans are a strange breed," replied the mermaid in her unusual rhyming voice. Jack put the ring back into his pocket. He wasn't afraid of this creature now, he felt powerful whilst he had the ring.

"Go and bring me some treasure. I know ye have it see and you can have yer ring back!" Jack ordered.

"I will do your bidding, for you hold my ring. The things you desire I must bring." The mermaid dived down into the water, her large fishy tail breaking the surface was the last thing Jack saw of her. The water was quiet once more.

......

It was colder now and Jack had waited nearly an hour before he caught sight of something gliding through the waves towards his rock. Jack was shivering, he was soaking wet from sea spray and slightly annoyed at having to wait so long. The now familiar face of Melusa broke the surface and she cast a heavy pouch onto Jack's rock.

"I hope you are pleased with what I have brought, for these many humans died, and many fought." Jack scooped up the heavy pouch, he weighed it in his hands.

"Ooh! What have ye brought me my lovely!" he said as he yanked open the string. Jack peeked inside then tipped out some of the contents into a cupped hand. A mixture of old gold coins and pearls filled his hand. "Ooh!. . . ooh! Very nice. . . very nice!" Jack danced a little jig on his rock in excitement.

"Now honour thy word man of the land, release unto me that what was made for my hand." The mermaid held out a delicate hand to Jack.

"Eh? No, no my lovely, this aint enough see. I want more, more like these I do!"

"Time never changes the men of the land, fighting, death, and greed is all they understand." Melusa said and she scowled once more. Jack threatened that she would never see her ring again unless she brought him more treasures. So, she did. After three more pouches were hurled onto the rock Jack refused to hand over the ring a final time.

"I still want more, I know you have it see and I want it. This lot's heavy, can't carry no more. I will be back tomorrow night and you will bring me more diamonds and gold, right?" Melusa's tail came up and she used it to propel herself away from the rock and out to sea.

"I must do your bidding for you have my ring. The things you desire I must bring," sang Melusa as she disappeared from sight. Jack gathered his bounty and made his way back to the sand. In a couple more hours it would be daylight and he had to get back home. Somewhere far out at sea Jack could hear the haunting singing of the mermaid of Siren's Dunes. His mermaid now.

Chapter 9
The ring was gone

Sophie woke up to the muffled sounds of crying. The crying was coming from downstairs and Sophie recognised it to be her mother. It was early morning. Sophie got out of bed and dressed herself quickly, then went downstairs. Sophie followed the sobbing and entered the kitchen. Helen was sitting at the kitchen table and Tom was comforting her.

"Mum, Dad, what's wrong?"

"I don't want you to worry love, but we've had a break in, sometime last night I think," answered Tom.

"A break in! You mean a burglary? We've been burgled?" gasped Sophie.

"Yes, whoever it was, was disturbed I think, because he didn't take much, just your mother's jewellery we think."

"Oh my god! Is Mum alright?"

"Yes love, I'm fine, just a bit upset. I had some very precious things in my jewellery box, wedding rings and stuff from your Nan. I can't believe it's gone!" Sobbed Helen.

"Shouldn't we telephone the police or something?" asked Sophie.

"Already done. They'll be sending an officer round shortly," said Tom and he poured a cup of tea for Helen.

"Gosh!" Sophie didn't really know what to say.

"The thief went into our room undetected, you better check your stuff love, see if anything is missing." Sophie did what Tom had said and she went to her room.

Sophie didn't have an awful lot of stuff with her on this holiday, just her game console that was still in its drawer by the bed, and her pocket money which amounted to a grand total of six pounds. It was still in the drawer too. Hardly worth stealing if you're a burglar she thought. Then Sophie had a horrible feeling. Her mum's jewellery was taken. The only jewellery Sophie owned was a necklace that she was still wearing, and the mermaid's ring.

Frantically Sophie searched for the ring. She looked under her pillow, in all the drawers, even under the bed. The ring was nowhere.

"Oh, where did I leave it?" she said out loud, exasperated. She had an idea and rummaged through her jeans pockets. Still the ring was missing. Sophie thought hard about what she had done the previous night. She had got into bed with her book and she had been wearing the ring. The ring had begun to comfort her somehow, it felt warm on her finger and if she thought about it, she could feel a slight pulse, as though the ring was alive and contained a tiny heart beating away. Fearing nightmares, she remembered that she had slipped off the ring and had placed it onto the cover of her book on the bedside cabinet.

The book was still there, but there was no sign of the ring. Sophie had come to the conclusion that the burglar had stolen it. She had no idea why anyone would steal it; it didn't look particularly valuable. Even her mother thought it was a bit of old sea glass. But the fact is it was gone, and they had been burgled. Sophie thought about what her dad had said. He said that nothing apart from her mum's jewellery box had been taken. So perhaps the burglar was looking specifically for jewellery, maybe even for a particular ring. Sophie hated her next thought, but it popped into her head before she could do anything about it. What if the burglar was looking for the mermaid's ring?

......

The police officer came around to the cottage rather promptly. Tom opened the door and the policeman was invited in. The police officer began writing a report on the burglary. Tom and Helen tried to tell him everything they could about how the thief got in and what exactly was stolen. Helen became tearful again when she read out her inventory of stolen jewellery. The police officer made a detailed list of all the missing items.

"Did any of the jewellery have any distinctive markings?" The police officer asked Helen. Sophie thought about the mermaid's ring and the engraved word '*Melusa*' but she said nothing fearing they wouldn't take her loss seriously. Helen told the police officer about her wedding ring and that hers and Tom's initials were engraved onto it.

"Good, that should make it easy to identify should we recover these items. Now, I will have to ask you to provide some fingerprints for elimination against any unaccountable or suspicious marks I may find on these premises." Tom, Helen, and Sophie all gave samples of their fingerprints and the police officer examined the cottage inside and out. When the police officer returned to the kitchen he looked rather pleased with himself.

"I managed to get some good prints from the kitchen window that would seem to be the place where the culprit gained access to this property," said the officer and he showed Tom before he sealed them up in a funny looking envelope. "I would now like to call at a few of the other houses in the street, see if anyone saw anything suspicious, then I will pop back and have a little chat before I return to the station."

The police officer called at three houses and a shop. Sophie watched him through a front window. Most of the people he talked to shook their heads only one man who owned the shop on the corner seemed to have something to tell of interest to the police officer, Sophie saw him writing something down before returning to their cottage. The police officer Told them that he would keep them informed of how the enquiry progressed and would let them know if someone is charged and the crime cleaned up. The officer also took time to point out to Tom and Helen all the security weaknesses at the cottage that needed attention. Tom explained that he would talk to the owner of the cottage before they left Siren's Dunes. Before the police officer left the cottage,

Sophie asked him what the man at the shop had told him.

"Oh, yes the shopkeeper said that he saw someone loitering about up and down the street for a while. He said he seemed to be acting suspicious."

"Did he get a description?" asked Helen.

"Not really, he said it was dark, but you never know, something else may crop up," the police officer said as he climbed into his car. Sophie watched the police car disappear down the road until it was out of sight.

......

Old Jack sat at his eating table in his house. The table was filled with the sparkling treasure that he had taken from the mermaid the previous night. Neat piles of gold, pearls, diamonds and silver trinkets were neatly set out and Jack was scribbling a full list of everything he had gained.

"Oh my giddy aunt! I'll soon be a very rich Jack!" Jack chuckled to himself. On the centre of the table stood Helen's jewellery box. The lid was open and Jack had some of Helen's possessions in a separate little pile. The contents of Helen's box in no way matched the splendour of the things the mermaid had brought him. In fact, Jack had scarcely examined Helen's things, favouring instead to paw the piles of mermaid gems some the size of boiled sweets. Jack took the mermaids ring out of his pocket. "Ah me lovely. What beauties will ye bring Old Jack tonight eh?" Jack placed the ring into Helen's jewellery box, his box now, and closed the lid. Jack yawned and stretched. "Need some shut eye I do, if I is to be up all night again." Jack fell heavily onto a little bed in the corner of the room and soon he was fast asleep and snoring for England.

......

Sophie had decided that she would go out shopping leaving her parents in the cottage to mull over what had happened to them the night before. There was no reason for them all to mope about the place and Sophie had six pounds still to spend. Sophie collected the coins from the drawer in her room and then she noticed something. Lying on the floor next to the wall with the window was a small red plastic torch. Sophie picked it up. She didn't remember bringing a torch, or even owning one such as this. Maybe it belonged to the previous family who stayed at the cottage. But then Sophie had another thought. What if the burglar dropped it?

Sophie examined the torch. The switch was pushed into the 'On' position, but there was no light. Sophie guessed rightly that the batteries must be flat. She decided to keep the torch and show it to her parents. As Sophie entered the living room she saw Helen still looking upset. She decided to forget showing them the torch for the time being.

"I'm just going to the shops Mum, won't be long," said Sophie trying to sound cheerful for her mother's benefit.

"Okay love, don't be too long though and be careful of the road, the people round here drive like maniacs!" Helen said herself trying to sound more optimistic.

"I will, bye," said Sophie as she closed the door behind her.

......

Sophie took her time, dawdling along the high street and peering into each and every shop window. She had no idea what she was looking for, but she knew she needed to spend some money to make herself feel better for having lost the mermaid's ring. Buying stuff always made Sophie feel better. After she had lost Kooler, Sophie had asked to have most of her savings from her bank account, and she had gone out with her mother and spent it on books, DVD's and computer games. It had worked for a while and she remembered that.

Sophie found herself looking into the most unusual shop window she had ever seen. The shop was called *'The Crystal Pentagram'* and apparently stocked everything that a sorceress need desire, or so the sign above the door stated. There were crystal balls, a multitude of fortune cards, candles of all shapes and colours. Sophie could hardly take it all in. She was about to walk on from the shop when she caught sight of a familiar face within. Examining a collection of strange necklaces hanging near the doorway stood Izabela the fortune teller from the funfair.

Sophie turned away from the shop doorway quickly when Izabela looked up from the rack of trinkets. It was not because she was afraid Izabela would recognise her and ask her if she had done as she advised regarding the mermaid's ring. No. Sophie suddenly had a terrible notion. Apart from her parents, there was only one other person who knew about the existence of the ring. Izabela. In an instant, Sophie had concluded that it must have been Izabela, or at least someone working for her that had burgled their cottage last night. Izabela must have the mermaid's ring. Sophie scampered away from The Crystal Pentagram, she had no idea where she was hurrying to exactly, but she had to get as far away from Izabela for the time being until she had come up with her plan. Sophie intended to get the mermaid's ring back.

Chapter 10
Lon

The fortune booth looked deserted. The door was closed, and there was a sign fixed to the largest of the glass panes. *'CLOSED FOR LUNCH, BACK AT 2'* Sophie read the sign. She had seen Izabela at The Crystal Pentegram about fifteen minutes ago. But she wasn't wearing a watch and she had no idea what time it actually was. She thought that she would look through the window of the booth whilst Izabela was out; she might be able to spot the ring.

Pressing her head against the door pane, Sophie peered inside the booth. It was gloomy inside and the window was a moulded glass of some kind that was difficult to see through, and the lace curtains made it even harder. Determined, she cupped her hands around her temples to block off any annoying light as she tried again to see inside. Sophie's heart raced. The door to the fortune booth wasn't locked. Her weight had forced the door open and she fell into the booth. She got to her feet as quickly as possible. She looked around but nobody was watching her. She rushed out of the booth and walked briskly away towards a bench positioned opposite the booth. She sat down. The door to the fortune booth swung gently in the breeze and its curtain fluttered, invitingly.

Sophie wished she had worn her watch. She nervously glanced up and down the funfair for a sighting of Izabela. Izabela could not be seen anywhere. Sophie realised this was her only chance to get the ring back, after all it could hardly be stealing if the ring was stolen from her she thought. She left the bench and slowly made her way back over to the booth. She closed the door tightly when she was in then she began to quickly look for the mermaid's ring amongst all of Izabela's clutter. There were so many little boxes arranged about the place. She opened all of them but none contained the ring, just different kinds of fortune cards. Then she saw something promising. On a little shelf at the back of the booth was a ceramic hand. Each shiny white finger held many different rings. Sophie examined all of them, but the mermaid's ring wasn't amongst them. Frustrated at finding nothing, Sophie sighed.

"Oi! Oi you!" A boy had entered the booth. He looked older than she was, although not by much and he had an angry face. "What are you doing in here? Nicking?" the boy asked barring the door. Sophie was taken by surprise by the whole thing and was dumbstruck. "Turn out your pockets, go on!" Shouted the boy. Sophie didn't know what to do, she had been caught in Izabela's booth and she was terrified.

"I said empty your pockets!"

"Okay, okay," replied Sophie and she began placing the few objects she was carrying onto the central table. Suddenly another figure stepped through the doorway. It was Izabela. Izabela took in the situation quickly.

"Lon, what's going on? Why is this girl here?"

"She's a tealeaf Mam, I caught her," answered Lon proudly.

"No I'm not! You are the thieves," shouted Sophie.

"Just hold on a minute. I know you, don't I?" Izabela stared at Sophie for a moment. "Yes, the girl with the unusual hair. You came here with your parents. I read your mother's fortune didn't I?" Sophie nodded. "But I don't understand. Why are you in my booth?"

"She's a thief Mam, I told you! I saw her come in, and I caught her looking through all your stuff an' that." Lon said exasperated. "I just nipped out, for a minute Mam honest, I think I must have forgot to lock the door."

"I was not! Thieving that is, I. . . I was looking for my ring," said Sophie defiantly.

"Ring? Yes, I remember. You had a Siren's ring child, didn't you?"

"Yes, I had it, but it was stolen. Our house was broken into last night. I thought you took it." Tears welled up in Sophie's eyes; she began to feel scared now of what Izabela would do to her.

"A siren's ring! You've got a siren's ring!" cried Lon in amazement.

"What on earth led you to believe it was I who burgled your house? I don't even know where you are living child." Izabela shook her head confused.

"You are the only one who knew about the mermaid's ring, apart from Mum and Dad. It had to be you." Sophie now began to sob.

"I can assure you it wasn't me who took the ring dear." Izabela put an arm around Sophie and they both sat at the table. Sophie wiped away her tears feeling more foolish by the second.

"What are you doing Mam? We should phone the old Bill!" said Lon in disbelief.

"I don't think so Lon. This child is no bandit."

"But...but...oh Mam," gasped Lon and he slumped down into a seat at the table. Izabela locked the door to her booth and put up a closed sign. Then she asked Sophie to tell her everything that had happened. Sophie related the previous night's events.

"Oh, I told you to take the ring back where you found it didn't I," said Izabela sternly. Sophie just nodded, "I knew that ring would bring bad luck, no mortal soul should have it see!" Izabela asked Lon to make them all a cup of tea, and she then opened a tin of biscuits. "Have your parents told the police?"

"Yep, they came around this morning. Got fingerprints." Sophie felt better now for the cup of sweet tea.

"Do the police have any idea who it was?" Asked Izabela desperate to help Sophie.

"No, not really," said Sophie, but then she got an idea. "Oh, I just thought!"

"What child?"

"Remember when I was last here, with my parents I mean?"

"Yes, what of it?"

"Well you said that you can do sycosmeny or something!" Izabela gave Sophie a puzzled stare, "you said you can hold an object in your hand and tell who it belonged to! You did it with my sea ring remember?"

"Ah! Psychometry child. Yes, I do have that peculiar gift. Why do you ask?"

"Because I have something I think belonged to whoever burgled our house!" Sophie leaned over the table to the small collection of belongings she had fished out of her pockets. She picked up the plastic torch, "I found this in my room this morning. It doesn't belong to us." Sophie put the torch down on the table in front of Izabela.

"Wicked!" said Lon delighted.

"Can you see who burgled our house?" Sophie asked Izabela.

"I don't know, it doesn't always work you know, but I will try." Izabela picked up the torch, and she held it tightly in-between both her hands. "Ah! Yes, I can see!" cried Izabela.

"What? What can you see Mam?" Lon asked excited. Izabela had her eyes shut tightly.

"A man, old and crafty he is, pushing something. A trolley, no, a dust cart. He cleans the streets, locally. He was born in this town. John, no Jacob, no Jack! Jack is his name. He thinks constantly of money. Greed is his one true overwhelming desire." Izabela placed the torch back onto the table, she rubbed her forehead. "I have to stop now, too strong the emotions were."

"That was wicked Mam! Do you mean Old Jack, Old Jack the binnie?" said Lon.

"Old Jack who?" Sophie asked. Izabela opened her eyes, she looked tired now.

"There is a local man, he cleans the fair, and a bit of a shifty slyboots he is. Nobody has anything to do with him really. But you must keep away from him."

"Surely, we have to do something. He burgled our house!"

"I know what I saw, whilst holding the torch, but that isn't proof enough not even for the police."

"But if we tell the police, tell them what you can do," Sophie pressed on.

"They will just laugh at us, at you. They wouldn't believe in psychometry," Izabela said glumly. Sophie sighed.

"You see, it wasn't just the mermaid's ring that he took. He stole some stuff from my Mum, things she loved."

"Oh. I am sorry about that. But like I said, without proof."

"I know. It just isn't fair," sighed Sophie. Izabela got up from the table and unlocked the door.

"I think you should go home now. Take the torch to the police if you want, but I doubt it would do any good."

"Well thanks for helping me, and I am sorry for thinking that you. . . you know."

"That's okay, I hope it all works out for your folks," said Izabela as she opened the door for Sophie. Sophie said her goodbyes and she left Izabela's booth.

"Hey, hang on! Wait up!" Lon caught up with Sophie as she was leaving the funfair gates.

"Oh, Lon it's you. What do you want?"

"Well I just had this sound idea, about how we, I mean you, could get your ring back!"

"How?"

"Well it's a bit tricky like, and you might need help."

"I don't understand Lon."

"Can I show you something first, it's about sirens, well mermaids, Mam likes to call them sirens," Lon blushed a little.

"What is it?"

"Well, I feel like a right ponce, but I've got a scrap book, about mermaids. You know, newspaper cuttings, old pictures and stuff. I've been collecting them for ages. Some people think only girls are interested in mermaids, but I think they're wicked too!"

"Oh. I would like to see it Lon," Sophie looked at Lon now properly, he had short very dark ruffled hair, and his eyes were a light brown. Sophie even thought that she rather liked him.

"Sound. You can come to our house, it's only over there," Lon pointed to a small pink house on the corner of the street that led up to Sophie's holiday cottage. Sophie agreed. Lon seemed like a nice boy, she could usually tell and was seldom wrong about people.

Chapter 11
The scrapbook of mermaids

Lon's house was very nice inside, not half as weird as she had imagined it to be. Somehow, she had expected to find all kinds of mystical ornaments and curiosities. Instead the house was as near normal as you could get. Lon went into the kitchen.

"Can I get you a drink?" Lon asked.

"Yes please, I'm parched." Lon returned with two tall glasses of Lemonade.

"Lemo's all we've got."

"That's fine really." Sophie sat down on a large plump beige sofa and Lon opened a drawer on a tall corner unit and produced his scrapbook.

"Gosh! It looks so thick. You must have been collecting stuff for ages," said Sophie astounded.

"I have, since I was five I think."

"But why mermaids Lon?"

"I don't really know, suppose it's me Mam really. She used to walk me along the beach, sing old songs, nursery songs about mermaids, and tell me stories like," Sophie took the scrap book from Lon and laid it on her knees. She carefully turned its pages. The book was crammed with so many pictures and articles all relating to Siren's Dunes and the mystical creatures from where it derived its name. There was one photograph, very old. Lon explained that he had found it in an old book and had cut it out along with its explanation. Sophie read the photograph's text out loud.

"A picture taken by local surgeon Doctor Frederick Fairbrother in eighteen hundred and ninety-two. The photograph allegedly shows one of the famous mermaids of Siren's Dunes. Doctor Fairbrother was caught up in the new craze of photography and was trying to capture a typical sunset when he saw the creature swimming off shore. Gosh!" Sophie studied the old picture, all that could be made out was a blurry shape on the surface of the water that resembled a head and shoulders.

"It's not the only picture, look!" Lon turned the pages of his scrapbook with uncanny precision. The page he presented showed more photographs of mermaids. Some were remarkably clear, and not very old. "People have been seeing mermaids around this coast for ages. Me Mam said she even saw one once. But I haven't. Love to I would!"

"I think I have, but in a dream," Sophie said thoughtfully.

"Well that doesn't count really does it?"

"I don't know, I don't really remember the dream only bits, but I was wearing my ring at the time." Lon took the scrap book away from Sophie again and sifted through its pages.

"Here. Is that like your ring?" Lon pointed to a black and white sketch of what Sophie recognised as being her ring.

"Yes. That's my ring, I don't believe it!"

"Well this drawing was made by a superstitious fisherman. He caught a really big fish, and he found this ring in its belly. He believed it to be a mermaid's ring and he kept the ring as a lucky charm for years, but eventually he threw it back into the sea. He said it was dangerous. This drawing was printed in the local papers years ago. I found it in the archives of the library." Sophie studied the ring carefully. The details were similar all for one thing.

"See the middle part of the ring, see the pearly thing?" Sophie showed Lon.

"Yep, I can see it."

"Well on my ring there was a word scratched around the pearl, it said Melusa, I think. This ring has another word. Zaden." Lon looked puzzled.

"What does it mean?"

"Well I never thought about it until now, but I think it might be a name. Possibly the names of the mermaids who the rings belong to."

"Wicked!" said Lon excited and he began making notes in the margin of his scrapbook. "When you had the ring, did it do anything? I mean, did it seem special or magic or anything?" Sophie decided that she would tell Lon everything about the ring, he really did seem interested and he probably wouldn't laugh at her either.

"Well whenever I wore the ring it felt strangely hot."

"Hot? What exactly was it made from?"

"I don't really know. It wasn't metal. It looked like glass of some kind. I think it was some kind of crystal. Like those," Sophie pointed to a small display cabinet in the corner of the room. On one of the shelves were a collection of semi-precious stones and crystals.

"Those are me Mam's. She collects them," said Lon before adding some more notes to his scrap book.

"There was something else about the ring. Something really weird." Lon gave Sophie his complete attention.

"Did it do something really wicked?"

"Sort of. You see I was on the beach and I was wearing the ring. I dipped my hand into a rock pool, I was actually trying to pick up a crab. When the ring touched the water, it began to glow!"

"Wicked! What did it look like?"

"As though the whole ring was a light bulb and someone switched it on!"

"So it was magical."

"There was something else too."

"What?"

"The pearly thing in the centre of the ring began to flicker, to flash. And then I could hear some singing. It was coming from way out at sea I think." Lon's mouth had dropped open as his brain absorbed all the facts Sophie had related. "That's all I saw. The ring was stolen soon after."

"This is the best thing I've ever heard. We've got to get it back!" shouted Lon.

"Yes, but how?"

"I have an idea." Lon said and he replaced his scrap book in the drawer and produced a thick telephone directory. "You see we know who stole your ring, it was old Jack the binnie. I know his full name. Jack Chenes. We all used to call him,

Mr Cheese, because he mings a bit you know." Sophie giggled. "Well if he has a phone we can find his address in here." Sophie thought it was a good idea and Lon began to seek old Jack amongst the legions of names in the book. "Chase, Chatersby, Chealer, ah! Here we are, J.W. Chenes. Six Long Drop road. Got im!" Lon wrote down the address on a scrap of paper.

"How can we be sure it's the right Jack?" Sophie asked.

"We can go there now, if we can just get a glimpse of him we'll know." Sophie wasn't sure. It sounded risky and she thought she ought to be getting back home. She didn't want her parents to start worrying about her, not so soon after the break in.

"I'm not sure Lon, I've been out all day. Maybe tomo–"

"It's not far, only a ten-minute walk." Lon was eager to investigate six Long Drop Road.

"Okay then, just a quick look." Sophie felt a rush of tingling excitement as she left Lon's house to begin their adventure.

Chapter 12
Six Long Drop Road

The house was very old. At some time in its past it had looked quite attractive, but now its white washed front was all covered with an invading cloak of ivy, and its door and window frames were shabby and worn. A crooked path led from the ruin of a front wall to the door. Lon read the number on the front door. It was an old horseshoe bent into the rough shape of a number six.

"What do we do now Lon?" Sophie and Lon were loitering on the pavement outside the house. There were two tall and very overgrown bushes within what remained of the front garden. Lon and Sophie were using them as shields so they could not be seen from within the house.

"We could knock on the door but he hates me, along with most of the other kids in the town. He would probably chase me away or worse." Lon said thoughtfully.

"I could knock." Sophie volunteered but felt scared all the same.

"No, he might recognise you from when he was in your house. He may have been watching you and your folks for a while." Lon had an idea. "I know, you crouch behind the wall, I'll knock and hide behind that big bush."

"That's bonkers! He'll see us for sure."

"Maybe, but we can leg it! At least we'll know we have the right house." Before Sophie could say anything else, Lon was creeping up the path to the front door.

Sophie tucked herself away behind the wall and spied on Lon through a large gap where a brick once existed. Lon stood in front of the front door. He paused for a moment making sure he had thought his plan out sensibly. Lon rapped loudly then sprinted to a crouching position behind the tall bush. Sophie's heart was pounding in her chest as she nervously glanced from Lon to the front door. Nothing happened. "Again," whispered Lon. But as he stood up they heard the sound of heavy bolts being slid back behind the front door. Seconds later the door was swung open.

Jack had an expression on his face that said he was expecting to see somebody at his front door. But there was nobody to be seen. Jack scanned his garden and the street beyond. Sophie held her breath. Lon crouched very still.

"Bloody kids! Be off with yer. Bloody stupid nuisance." Jack cursed. Jack turned to go back inside his house but then stopped. Lon's foot had been covering a dried fallen twig from one of the large bushes in Jack's garden, under the pressure it had snapped. Jack heard the snapping twig and whirled around in his doorway. Sophie glanced at Lon's face as her heart skipped a beat. "Hidin' in me garden are ye?" roared Jack as he leaped out from the doorway.

"Leg it!" cried Lon and he sprung to life jumping over Jack's dilapidated wall. Sophie joined Lon and they ran fast down the street away from Jack's house.

"I'll catch ye, next time, bloody brats! You see if I don't!" Jack slipped back into his house and the door was closed with a loud bang, followed by the sound of many securing bolts.

Sophie caught up to Lon around the next street corner. He was leaning against a shop window, giggling as he caught his breath.

"Wh–cough! What's funny?" asked Sophie. She stood with her hands on her knees and she was bent over gulping for air.

"Did you see im? Silly old Mr Cheese! Thought he'd catch us I did," said Lon still laughing.

"So did I. I nearly died. Gosh I was scared Lon." Sophie said. She stared at Lon with a serious expression. Lon stopped laughing for a moment and tried to make his face serious too. Both Sophie and Lon burst into laughter together.

"Sorry Sophie can't help it. Phew! That was a good laugh that was."

"I am right in thinking that was, Jack am I? The man who we think took my ring?"

"Yep, that was definitely, Mr Cheese all right!"

"So what do we do now?" Sophie asked Lon to see if he had anymore crazy ideas lined up. After a short while thinking quietly, Lon announced that he had a plan.

"I will watch Jack's house tonight. If I see him leave it, I will follow him to see where he is going. He might go to the pub or something I dunno. Anyway, when the house is empty I'll come and get you and we can try to get the ring back."

"Lon don't be silly. I would never be able to go out at night, not on my own. My mum and dad would never allow it."

"Look, my Mam wouldn't like it either, but she need not know. I will go to bed early then sneak out. I've done it before!" Lon smiled.

"I couldn't do that, could I?" Sophie doubted she could be that devious.

"You want your ring back don't you?"

"Well yes."

"This is the only way. Look Sophie, you are a mate, I like you, I will try to get your ring back on me own if I have to. But, I'd rather you came with me." Sophie was stunned to hear Lon talk the way he did. He said she was his mate, his friend. Sophie didn't have all that many friends back home, and especially not boys. Lon had also said that he liked her, and that made her feel somehow good inside.

"Okay. If you are sure it will work."

"Hey, trust me. It will work." Lon looked pleased with Sophie's decision to accompany him on their next adventure.

"Then what's the plan Lon?"

"Like I said, I will watch his house first. When it's empty I'll come to get you, but you must tell me where you are staying, and which is your bedroom window. I will throw something at your window, so make sure you are in your room all night, and be listening."

"And then what? We go to Jack's house and break in?"

"Sure. Listen Sophie, Jack's the thief. We're only getting your stuff back aren't we?"

"Suppose. But still, breaking into a house is wrong Lon."

"I know it is, but like I said, it is the only way."

"Ok Lon. I will wait for you tonight."

"Great, see you later then." Lon trotted away down the street leaving Sophie still at the shop, he turned to wave at her. Sophie waved back then realised she hadn't told him where she lived.

"Lon, wait!" Sophie shouted, "we are staying at Gull Cottage!"

"I know it! It's the white house right?" Lon answered.

"Yes, my bedroom is at the front of the house, it has blue curtains. I will leave my light on!"

"Okay, see you later." Lon waved a final time then disappeared around the next corner. Sophie began her walk back to the cottage. She thought about the night ahead, Lon's plan worried her, but she was happy about seeing him again later.

Chapter 13
An adventure begins

When Sophie returned to Gull Cottage Tom and Helen were waiting for her. Tom had decided they would all leave Siren's Dunes for the rest of the day and travel by car to the neighbouring town of Twilight Bay. There was a castle there as well as other interesting attractions. Sophie couldn't think of any reason to say why she wouldn't like to go and Helen had already made them all a picnic to take with them.

Sitting in the back of the car Sophie hoped they would all be back at Gull Cottage that night in time for when Lon came to collect her. She would hate to let him down. He would think that she had chickened out of the whole thing. Helen was looking forward to getting away from the cottage for a while; a change of scenery would surely cheer her and Tom up after the break in. As the car pulled away from the cottage Sophie glanced at her watch, it was something she would be doing many times during the remainder of the day and night. It was three pm.

……

It was near the end of August and the evenings had begun to roll in quickly at Siren's Dunes. It was eight thirty and already dark. Lon was back outside Jack's house. He was watching the house from the corner of the street. Occasionally he would move away from his spot to avoid a group of noisy partygoers on their way to one of the disco bars on the sea front. But he never took his eyes off the house for long.

Lon could see that Jack was in as light spilled out through gaps in the curtains on the lower part of the house. Not only were the nights drawing in quicker now, the wind had discovered a new and chilly breath. Lon was without a jacket; it was a habit carried over from the long hot summer that was now fading away. Lon shivered and wished he had brought his coat.

Inside number six Long Drop Road, Jack was preparing for another night of gathering riches brought to him by his beautiful servant of the sea Melusa. Tonight, Jack had brought down a large leather bag from his attic. He intended on filling the bag with as much gold and jewels as Melusa could bring in a single night.

Jack opened a cupboard and lifted out Helen's jewellery box. He laid the jewellery box down on his supper table and unclasped the lid. The mermaid's ring sparkled at Jack from within the box and Jack picked up the ring and placed it into his trouser pocket. Jack poured himself a large glass of rum from an old bottle he kept on top of his mantel piece, "ah! This'll warm us up till the time's right." Jack said and he sank himself into his favourite armchair slurping his drink.

......

Sophie couldn't be more bored. For one whole hour, she had been sitting in the beer garden of the Sea horse pub with her parents. They had had their picnic at the pub and now Tom was enjoying a glass of beer. Sophie glanced at her watch

75

again, it was nine o'clock. Helen had just returned to the garden table carrying a cup of coffee. Sophie squirmed in her seat. It was really late and her mum would surely take ages to finish the coffee. Sophie decided it was time to act.

"Mum, Dad, I feel really tired. Can we go home now?" she asked whilst faking a yawn.

"It's unusual for you to be tired love. Are you feeling alright?" Helen asked concerned. She knew how full of energy Sophie always seemed, and at home it was sometimes something of a battle to get her up the stairs to bed.

"I'm fine Mum, just whacked out. Can't wait for my bed."

"Sure, soon as your dad and I have finished our drinks we will head back to the cottage. Shan't be long love." Helen took a large gulp of her coffee then wished she hadn't, it was very hot. Sophie looked at her watch again, it was one minute past nine now. Sophie could picture Lon standing outside their cottage, trying to rouse her attention. She felt awful for letting him down. Helen took another gulp of steaming coffee when Sophie faked yet another yawn.

......

The lights blinked out. Now the whole house was in darkness. Lon had been stepping up and down the kerb outside Jack's house; the simple exercise has kept him warm during his nightly vigil. Lon stopped his activity and crouched low. He could hear the heavy bolts sliding back behind the front door and then it swung open. Jack stood on the doorstep fiddling with a bunch of keys. The door was closed and Jack locked the door then set off down his path.

Lon watched Jack cross the street. He was carrying a large leather shoulder bag. Lon kept his distance and followed Jack as he strode along the high street.

"Bet he's off to the pub," Lon whispered to himself. But he was wrong. Jack ambled past the Mermaid public house on the corner without so much as giving it a glance. Lon wondered where on earth he was going to and continued to shadow him.

Lon had followed Jack all the way down to the promenade and now Jack seemed to be heading out to the beach. Lon trailed behind Jack as he approached a set of corroded iron steps leading down to the sand. Jack descended the steps and Lon watched as he shuffled along the sand towards an outcrop of barnacle encrusted boulders that spilled into the sea itself. Happy that Jack was up to something that was sure to keep him occupied for some time, Lon raced off to collect Sophie from Gull cottage.

Nine forty-five. Sophie kept an eye on the passing of each and every minute during the drive home. Helen was driving this time, usually Tom drove the car but he had indulged himself in one or two beers at the Sea horse. Helen was a much slower driver than Tom.

"Won't be long now love, soon be home," Helen said. Sophie hoped they would. Lon didn't give her a time he would be at the cottage exactly, and in any case, it would only be if Jack went out. For all they knew Jack could be planning on spending the whole night indoors.

"How long Mum?"

"About ten minutes I think." Sophie sighed.

......

Lon searched for a small stone or twig in the front garden of Gull cottage. He settled for a small dried up seedpod instead, this would make less of a noise on the window pane he thought. Lon studied the front bedroom windows. There were two of them. Sophie said hers was the one with the blue curtains, but it was difficult to make out colours in the dark. She had also said that she would have her bedroom light switched on. Maybe she had forgot. Lon decided which curtains seemed blue in the gloom, and he cast the seedpod watching it hit the windowpane.

Lon collected the seedpod and used it time and again to alert Sophie to his presence in the garden, but she didn't appear at the window and the house remained quiet. Frustrated, Lon discarded the seedpod and scooped up a handful off gravel from a flowerbed nearest the house. He cast the gravel at Sophie's window creating the most tumultuous clattering sound that should have roused the entire house if it were occupied. Lon cringed at the noise and wished he hadn't thrown the gravel at all. Everything fell silent again.

"Typical. Typical girl!" cursed Lon in frustration. He felt let down by Sophie's apparent absence from the cottage. In fact, he couldn't believe she wasn't there. Maybe this was the end of their brief friendship he thought. Perhaps, she had merely been humouring him saying she would go with him tonight, when all along she had no intention of embarking on such a foolhardy adventure.

Lon decided he would go it alone. If Sophie didn't want her ring back, then he would have it. It would be the best item in his entire mermaid collection. What would old Jack Cheese want with it anyway? Lon cupped his hands around his mouth, "Sophie! Sophie! If you're in there, I just want you to know, I'm going now, to Jack's place. I'm gonna get the ring back! You know where to find me." Lon hissed in a low tone then left the garden of Gull cottage. He glanced back one final time to see an inert bedroom window. Lon ran off down the street, he had work to do and hoped he had the time in which to do it.

It was five minutes past Ten o'clock when Sophie saw Lon running past their car window. Sophie used the handle to wind the window down, but by the time she had done it, Lon was nowhere to be seen. Sophie felt mortified at the prospect of Lon being true to his word and calling for her. All she had done was let him down. She thought about it as the car came to a stop outside the cottage.

Once indoors Sophie rushed to the kitchen and poured herself a large glass of water. She then announced her immediate departure to her bed and went upstairs. In her room, she began to prepare for the night ahead. She fully intended to help Lon and began to work quickly.

First she changed into some warmer clothes, she had felt the coolness of this night whilst sitting in the beer garden eating dinner. Then she removed Jack's torch from a drawer and switched it on to test its power. The beam was still bright from when she had exchanged the batteries for some new ones she had inside an old game device she'd brought along. She slipped the torch into her Jeans pocket. Sophie pulled back her duvet cover and placed two pillows on the mattress. She then replaced the duvet and was pleased to see that she had created an illusion of somebody sleeping in the bed. But she wondered if it would fool her parents should they look in on her. It might do, if they didn't linger too long, and look too hard she thought.

Sophie opened her bedroom window and looked down towards the front door. She had thought about how she would get away unnoticed from the cottage during dinner and the journey home. Her bedroom overlooked the front door and above the door was a sloping canopy. Sophie guessed that she would be able to lower herself down from the window onto the canopy then jump down onto the path below. The front door was rather short, and the distance from the canopy to the ground was not too great. She knew she could easily make the jump. Sophie took a deep breath. It was now or never she thought.

Chapter 14
A drawer full of old gold coins

Old Jack Chenes was back on his small island of sea washed rocks. He remembered the last time he was here and how dark it was, and how spooky the mermaid had looked, his mermaid now. This time Jack had brought with him a small lantern. He wasn't normally afraid of the dark. The dark had been very useful to Jack over the years, as it acted as an aid to his nightly pilfering. But tonight, Jack would feel better sitting within the friendly glow from his lantern.

Jack lit the candle in the lantern box using a small silver cigarette lighter. Jack didn't smoke himself, he obtained the lighter during a spree of pick pocketing at the fair ground not so long ago, it looked nice and could come in handy he had thought. He reached into his pocket for the mermaid's ring.

This time Jack had attached some string to the ring. He dangled the ring into the somewhat turbulent waters. Immediately the ring burst into life. The dazzling green light that issued from the ring lit up the waters around the rocks where Jack sat. It was as though the ocean had become a vast aquarium and somebody had switched on a fluorescent light. Jack was amazed to see a variety of fish darting about in shoals below the surface breakers. Jellyfish were themselves illuminated by the rings green light, and Jack watched them dancing in the tidal current. Jack then became aware of a familiar sound.

The singing was distant at first but Jack instantly recognised it as belonging to his marine enchantress. Still dangling the ring in the water, Jack scanned the stretch of water before him. There she was. Almost dolphin-like she swam towards him. Jack removed the ring from the water, it felt very warm now; he shook it dry and slipped it into his pocket. There was a loud splash followed by the sight of a great fish tail breaking the surface of the water. Jack quickly reached within his leather bag for a silver flask.

"Who holds the ring and calls to me from my home beneath the sea?" The soft melodic voice rang out. Jack gulped a mouthful of rum from his silver flask and tossed it back into his leather bag. The lantern revealed the mermaid; she was using a hand to shield her eyes from the candles brilliance. Jack gasped when he saw her again. The mermaid was just as amazing as he had remembered. The same untamed long tresses of red and green hair, the sparkling complexion, and the burning yellow eyes. The lantern had enabled Jack to see some other things, things he hadn't noticed in the gloom the previous time. Her skin was dotted with barnacle like growths and small eel like creatures squirmed within her matted hair. The squirming eels made Jack feel sick and his face revealed his disgust. The mermaid used her wide fishy tail to splash water over the lantern putting out its flame.

"Oi yer sea witch!" cried Jack in fright.

"The fire box shines so bright, my eyes are not used to such a light," sang the mermaid.

"Tis me, old Jack. I want you to bring me something lovely, like the other night. I have yer ring see so you have to obey!"

"If for you more treasures I bring, will you give me back my ring?"

"I might, and then again, I might not. Just do as I say or you will never see your ring again!" Jack snarled.

"I must do your bidding for you have my ring. The things you desire I must bring." The mermaid turned in the water then dived down deep, her shining eyes were like small headlamps guiding her through the gloomy depths. Jack watched the lights fade as she swam forever further and deeper.

......

When Sophie reached Old Jack's house she lost her nerve and became scared for the first time. What if Lon had gone home annoyed at Sophie not waiting for him like she had promised? Maybe Lon had given up on her and had decided to give up on the mermaid's ring too. Sophie had another thought. What if Jack was in the house?

Sophie stood outside the house for a while. She watched the windows. They didn't look as though anybody was home, and she could see no flickering light from a television set or anything. Maybe Jack didn't own a television, or maybe he simply wasn't watching it tonight. Sophie crept up the path to the front door. Maybe Jack was sitting quietly inside his house waiting for her to come, ready to grab her. Sophie had begun to scare herself more.

The overgrown bushes and trees in Jack's garden were swaying slightly; they creaked as they rubbed together in the wind. Sophie imagined that she could see shadows amongst them, shadows that were Jack-shaped. Sophie shuddered. She decided she would creep around the back of the house just in case Lon was waiting for her, but she knew he wouldn't be really, not after she had let him down.

The back of Jack's house was as scruffy as the front. There was a lot of junk scattered about the place, old tires, fridges, a piano, a rusty car without any doors, and most peculiar of all there was an old red telephone box lying on its side. Sophie gingerly looked around. The house seemed just as deserted from the back as it did from the front. A mangy looking Tomcat jumped down from a piece of old corrugated iron fencing near to the telephone box. The moggy landed on an old tin can and sent it clattering to the floor. Sophie jumped with fright and slapped a palm to her mouth to muffle her cry of terror. The cat shot through her legs and disappeared behind her somewhere.

Sophie calmed herself down then decided enough was enough. She couldn't believe she was actually standing in somebody's back garden. What would she say if she was caught? Sophie was stopped from leaving the junkyard at the back of Jack's house. A small square piece of paper caught her eye. It was twisting in the wind along with some old leaves. Sophie bent down and picked it up. She instantly recognised it. It was from Lon's scrapbook. It was the picture of the other mermaid's ring, the one drawn by that superstitious fisherman. The fact that this picture was here meant only one thing. Lon was also here, or had been here at least.

Sophie saw that the Tomcat had reappeared. The cat ran up to the back door and Sophie watched in amazement as it revealed to her a sliding panel that it used to gain entrance to the house. Sophie realised then that it must be Jack's cat, and Jack had made it a cat flap of sorts, obviously not one you would buy in the shops. Sophie went over to the door and examined the cat flap. It was quite large. Large enough for her to crawl through. She poked her head in.

"Lon, Lon are you in there?" she whispered. She listened for a moment. There was nothing. Suddenly another voice answered her.

"Sophie? Sophie is that you?" Sophie recognised it as being Lon's voice, he had a funny accent. She still couldn't see anything only darkness. A light appeared. Torchlight guessed Sophie and it shone right in her face. Sophie closed her eyes.

"Oi!" she cried.

"Oh sorry Sophie, had be sure it was you." Lon's face appeared from out of the gloom. He had placed the torch underneath his chin and Sophie could now see him. "I thought you had chickened out. I can't believe you're here, that you came here on your tod." Lon said amazed.

"Well I said I was coming didn't I?"

"You weren't at your house. I came for you. I was throwing stuff at your window for ages." Sophie giggled.

"Sorry, I was with my mum and dad, they took me away from the town. We were late getting back."

"Well at least you're here now. Quick climb through, its sound. Jack's out." Sophie squeezed through the cat door.

Jack's kitchen was very basic. Just an old oven that looked like it hadn't been used in ages, a sink, and a stool. There were no cupboards or anything useful really. Sophie took her torch out of her pocket. She switched it on.

"I knew you were here," she said.

"How?"

"I found this." Sophie handed Lon the picture she had recovered from outside.

"God! I must have dropped it. What a twonk! I brought it to help me spot the ring if I found it."

"How long have you been here Lon, and more importantly, where is Jack?"

"Well, I waited outside the house for ages before Jack left. I followed him all the way to the beach. God knows what he's doing on the beach at this time of night. I left him there and came here. I spent a while trying to find a way in then I saw the cat door. Stupid of him really. I think I've been here for about half an hour, but I'm not sure." Sophie shone her torch around the kitchen. The beam came to rest on an old wall clock.

"It's ten to eleven!" gasped Sophie.

"Then I must have been here a bit longer than I thought. We'd best hurry. I haven't found your ring yet and he might come back soon." Lon led Sophie out of the kitchen and into the main living room of the house.

There were lots of old chests of drawers and bookcases full of more old junk. Sophie and Lon began to search each shelf and every drawer for the ring. Sophie spotted something on Jack's supper table.

"Lon, you were right, it's my mum's jewellery box. So, it was Jack!" Sophie examined the box, she had seen it so many times over the years. It was unmistakably her mother's box. Inside the box Sophie was pleased to find most of her mother's rings and necklaces intact. Now Sophie searched for her sea ring, she knew it had to here now.

"Hey Sophie look at these!" Lon shouted in excitement. Sophie put her mother's box back down on the supper table to see what Lon had found. Lon was standing in front of an open drawer. The drawer was filled with golden coins. Lon scooped some out and carried them in his hands over to the supper table. He let them spill onto the table top.

"Look at these coins Sophie, they are so heavy!" Lon held one of the glittering disks out for Sophie to examine. Sophie took the coin from Lon and studied its markings.

"It looks very old Lon, I think they are gold too. Look, there's a date on this one, seventeen twenty eight, it says!"

"What on earth is he doing with a drawer full of old gold coins?"

"I don't know, it is weird. They must be worth a fortune. Let's look for the ring and leave Lon." Sophie had decided they should hurry up or else be caught. She didn't imagine Jack or anybody would be too pleased having somebody nosing about their home and fiddling with their more than probable ill gained loot. Lon looked out of the window. The orange street lamps illuminated the road quite well. There was no sign of Jack yet.

"I can't see him coming, let's keep looking Sophie." Both Sophie and Lon resumed their searching.

Chapter 15
A golden crab

It was lonely on the rocks. Jack was sitting down, waiting for a sign of the mermaid's return. He had tried unsuccessfully to relight his lantern; the wick had become all brittle and he had snapped it off by mistake during his last attempt. Instead Jack amused himself with the mermaid's ring, he spun the ring upon the rock using his forefinger and thumb, watching the moonlight sparkle from it in an almost magical way.

It was the light that Jack saw first. A ghostly pale glow rising slowly towards the surface. Jack picked up the ring and got to his feet in time to see the mermaid's head emerge above the foam.

"Ah, me lovely Sea Hag, I mean, me beauty! What have ye brought old Jack then eh?" The mermaid lifted an arm and revealed a piece of old barnacle-encrusted rope. She held the rope out towards Jack. "Eh? What be this? No gold?" Jack took the rope from the mermaid, he realised that it was tied to something below the surface of the water, "oh! This be more like it. Is it a treasure chest me beauty? Or a gigantic pearl the size of me head!" Jack squawked as he hauled in his booty.

The end of the rope was tied around a wooden box. Jack dragged the box onto the rocks. There was no obvious way of opening the box so Jack took a sturdy pen-knife out of his pocket and used it to pry open the top which was pinned by heavy nails. The wood was soaked through and the lid came off easy. Jack peered inside. Instead of gold Jack saw a cluster of old bottles. "Eh? But where's me gold?"

"There are many treasures beyond those that shine. I have brought instead the finest wine," said the mermaid, and she gave Jack a beaming smile. Jack lifted one of the bottles out of the box and removed its cork using his pen-knife. Jack took a swig of the wine.

"You be right me pretty one, this ere wine's good, I'll give ye that I will, but good wine or no good wine, I want more gold. I know you have more gold see, and I want it!"

"I have brought you all of my treasures man of the land, you promised to give me back what belongs on my hand." The mermaid lifted her hand up to Jack, Jack felt a sudden burning sensation in his hand and he opened his clenched fist dropping the ring onto the rocks. The ring was burning white hot.

"Arrgh! Ye Sea Witch! Me blasted hand is on fire!" Jack yelped and he quickly fell to his knees plunging his hand into the cooling water. The mermaid closed in on Jack's hand and she grasped hold of it. Jack squirmed at the mermaid's cold touch. "Ere! What are ye doing?" cried Jack as he struggled to free his hand from the mermaid's grip.

"Look at the water, look at the sea. Try it yourself, come and swim with me." The mermaid's soothing rhyme lingered in Jack's ears.

"The water... yes. I'd like that I would." Jack looked deeper and deeper into the mermaid's burning eyes; he was slipping under her spell.

"I will show you a place full of magical things, where men like you could live like kings."

"Kings... yes I would like to see... to see..." Jack followed the mermaid's pull and braced himself for a plunge into the water that already licked at his shoes.

"Come... come... come," sang the mermaid.

"Stop! Stop you devil! I am the master, me, me, me!" Jack snapped out of his trance and wrenched back his hand. The mermaid scowled. "Oh, you nearly had me there you little witch, hook line and sinker," shouted Jack, he was angry. Jack searched for the sea ring he had dropped. The ring lay next to his left foot; it still looked hot. Jack held his foot over the ring. "Oh no, no, my little sea urchin. This ring belongs to me now and so do you. I could stamp on this ring see, smash it to bits! Would you like that me lovely eh?" The mermaid shook her head in answer to Jacks threat. "Good, then we understand each other eh? Now go fetch me more gold, or I will smash it!" The mermaid unhooked a leathery pouch from around her middle, she held it up for Jack to see.

"I have one last thing, all golden and pure. It's the best of the lot, I have no more." Jack snatched the pouch from the mermaid.

"Cor! It's heavy!" Jack fumbled with the pouch managing to open a heavy clasp. Jack's eyes lit up in delight when he saw what was inside. "Blimey!"

said Jack as he uncovered a fabulous, jewelled, solid gold crab. Jack turned over the heavy trinket and examined every diamond, ruby and sapphire that his hungry eyes could take in. "Ye are right. This ere is the best of the lot! Worth a fortune no doubt." Jack was delighted and he slipped the golden crab back in its pouch.

"My ring man of the land. You owe me that which belongs on my hand." The mermaid asked for the return of her ring once more.

"Oh no me lovely. I bet you have more things like this crab. A big golden starfish maybe eh?" The mermaid shook her head. "Like I said before, whilst I have yer ring you must obey me. I will be back tomorrow night. You will bring me more treasures." Jack left the rocks and made his way down to the sandy beach. The mermaid had allowed the sea to carry her away from the shore, she was smiling, a crafty smile before she disappeared below the surface. Jack was struggling with the box of wine, it was heavy, and so was the golden crab. Jack walked as fast as he could; he had to get home in a good time to save his arms from exhaustion.

Chapter 16
Jack's back

Sophie and Lon had searched relentlessly for the sea ring. They had left no drawer, cupboard or container untouched. The ring remained undiscovered. Sophie had guessed rightly that Jack must have the ring on his person. Lon still thought otherwise and had noticed a small door that led to a cubbyhole under the stairs.

"It's the only place we haven't looked Sophie. He might have put the ring in there."

"I think we should go Lon, we've been here absolutely ages, Jack's bound to be back home soon," said Sophie anxious to get away.

"I know, but one quick scope about and then we will leave. Promise." Sophie agreed and they opened the door that led to the space underneath the stairs. It was pitch black inside. Sophie switched on her torch. There were umbrellas, shoes, and a load of old coats strewn about. There was no obvious place where Jack would hide valuable items.

"It's no good in here Lon, I bet Jack has the ring with him. We should go." Sophie urged Lon.

"Okay, it's a shame we didn't find your ring. We'll never have another chance you know."

"I know Lon, but we tried. Let's get home before we are missed."

Sophie was the first one to leave the cubby-hole and as she slipped out into the hallway she heard something that made her heart leap into her mouth. The sound of a key being turned in the front door. Sophie backed up into the cubby-hole forcing Lon to retreat also.

"Oi! What are you doing?" said Lon after Sophie pushed him back inside.

"It's Jack, he's back!" answered Sophie as she closed the cubby-hole door. She held onto the handle tightly. Lon's eyes widened with fright when he heard the front door slam shut. Heavy boots plodded past Sophie's and Lon's hideout. They both held their breath until the boots had moved away. Sophie released her grip on the door handle.

"Oh Lon what are we going to do now?"

"I don't know. One thing's for sure, we're stuck in here now." Sophie felt tears begin to well in her eyes; she was so frightened.

Jack dumped the box of wine on to his supper table. He rubbed his back. It had been a gruelling walk home carrying all this stuff. Jack turned on a small gas fire and stood in front of it to warm himself up. He looked at the leathery pouch lying next to the box of wine. Jack picked up the pouch and took out the crab. He turned it over in his hand examining it more closely this time. It was a beautiful thing. The gold was so polished he saw his own grizzled mug staring back at him. "Cor, this will bring old Jack everything he wants. I could leave this trashy town for good. Be a millionaire!" Jack chuckled to himself. In his good humour, Jack took a bottle of wine out of the box. He removed the cork and began to swig from the bottle. Soon the wine had taken effect on Jack and he slumped into his favourite armchair.

......

Helen and Tom were sitting by the fire in Gull Cottage. It was a quarter to midnight and they were both feeling ready to hit the sack. It had become a chilly night, and Helen had decided to pop upstairs and put an extra blanket on their bed. Tom said he would make them both a drink of hot chocolate whilst she was upstairs. Helen had made up a warmer bed for her and Tom using some blankets that she found in a large chest in their bedroom. She took an extra blanket from the chest and decided to check on Sophie to see if she needed some extra warmth.

As Helen walked across the landing she felt a cool draught whooshing past her. The cold air made her skin goosepimply and she wondered where on earth it was coming from. The door to the empty bedroom was opening and closing in the draught. Helen opened the door to the spare room to check that the window was shut. It was and she closed the door firmly and made her way to Sophie's room.

Helen opened Sophie's bedroom door and was hit by a stream of cold air. "Goodness me!" she said and she saw that the bedroom window was open slightly. Helen glanced over at Sophie's bed. She saw the huddled lump under the duvet and crept over to shut the window. The cool winds had been rolling in from the sea all evening and now the room was icy cold.

Helen quietly unfolded the blanket she was carrying and draped it over the top of Sophie's bed. As she tucked the blanket in Helen realised that she couldn't see Sophie's head or her pillows. Alarmed, Helen pulled back the duvet to reveal the two pillows and the absence of Sophie herself. Helen panicked. "Tom! Tom!" she cried as she raced along the landing to the top of the stairs. "Oh Tom, quick it's Sophie!" Tom appeared at the bottom of the stairs and saw Helen blubbing almost hysterically as she descended.

"What's happened, what's wrong?" Tom asked.

"Sophie's gone! She's gone, oh what are we going to do?"

"Please calm down love, what do you mean Sophie's gone?"

"She's missing. Her bed is empty, and her window was open! She's gone Tom!"

"Oh my god!" Tom cried and he ran upstairs and checked out Sophie's room. Tom saw the bed with the pillows arranged to make it look as though Sophie was sleeping. He then searched the cottage from top to bottom; Helen was calling for Sophie all the while Tom searched. Tom gripped Helen by the shoulders "She's not in the house love, I will look outside." Tom opened the front door and ran outside. Helen could hear Tom shouting for Sophie in the street and with a trembling hand she picked up the telephone and began to dial for the police.

Chapter 17
Hiding under the stairs

Jack's eyes were feeling heavy; he placed an empty bottle of wine down on the floor next to his armchair. "Boris! Boris!" he called and moments later a ginger cat clambered through the cat-flap and made its way to Jack jumping onto his lap. The cat purred loudly as Jack fussed him. "Eh? Boris, we is rich me son, yes we is rich!" Jack waffled pie-eyed from the effects of the wine. Boris jumped off Jack's lap and on to the supper table. He sniffed at the box of wine and then became interested in the leathery pouch next to it.

Boris began to scratch at the pouch, and somehow managed to open its draw string revealing a golden claw. Boris leapt back from the pouch and began to hiss loudly, his whole body had become rigid. Jack dragged himself out of his armchair and staggered over to the table. "Wash matter Boris eh?" Boris was standing all arched. He used his paw to stab at the shiny claw that poked through the open pouch. "Nay Boris! Thish aint nout t'fear! Thish be our fortune Boris," slurred Jack and he took the golden crab out of the pouch. "Look Boris, a beauty, a real beauty it be!" Boris continued to hiss at the crab and he leapt off the supper table and trotted out into the kitchen and through the cat flap.

Jack stroked the golden crab and he began to sway unsteadily. "More to be desired are they than gold, yup! Than mush fine gold!" Jack dropped the crab clumsily and it fell heavily onto the supper table. His hand was sore and he turned his palm up to examine it with his blurry eyes. The mermaid's ring had branded a red mark into his palm when it had burned white hot at the beach. Jack took the ring out of his pocket and tossed it onto the supper table. Best out of his pocket he thought. "Oh me head!" Jack cried and he placed his hands over his face and fell back into his armchair. Within minutes he was snoring loudly.

Sophie and Lon had been sitting quietly underneath the stairs for about half an hour. They dared not move or talk above a whisper for fear of being caught. They had both heard Jack drop the golden crab onto the table. The crab was heavy and the noise was loud. They didn't know what the noise was but it told them that Jack was still awake and definitely in the lower part of the house. Sophie's torch had lost some of its brilliance and cast a pale orange circle on the floor of the hideout.

"My batteries are running out Lon," whispered Sophie.

"I have my torch. I won't use it, I'll save the batteries," replied Lon trying to sound more cheerful.

"Lon, what do you think he will do to us if he finds us here?"

"I suppose he'll be mad. Maybe he will just kick us out of the house."

"Yeah maybe. He might get the police, then we will be in trouble. We'll be burglars!"

"No, not old Jack. He's too shady. He must be up to all sorts. We both saw all that money in the drawers. The last thing Jack would do is get the police!"

"Yeah, you're probably right. I just wish, wish I wasn't here." Sophie almost let go of her tears. Lon put an arm around her.

"Hey, come on Sophie. It's an adventure. Our adventure. Tomorrow we will be back with our folks and this will just be a memory you'll see."

"I hope so." Sophie thought about what Lon said, about being back with their folks. Sophie really missed her mum and dad right now, and wished she were safely tucked up in her bed at the cottage. There was something that puzzled Sophie. She had met Lon's mother Izabela, but Lon had never talked about his father.

"Lon, I really am scared, and when I feel scared I think about my dad and my mum because I always know that they would always protect me if they could. Where's your dad Lon?" Sophie suddenly felt awkward about asking this question and when she saw Lon's saddened face in the gloom, she wished she hadn't.

"Me dad's dead Sophie." Sophie had not expected this answer and she felt terrible for bringing the whole matter up.

"Oh I'm sorry Lon, I had no idea."

"It's okay Sophie, you couldn't know. It was a few years ago now. I guess I've got used to it."

"It must be awful. How. . . how did he. . . "

"It's alright, you can say it. He died because he got sick, real sick. It was some kind of Leukaemia, the doctors said. The funny thing is, of all the things I could miss about him, the one thing I do miss is his laugh. He had a wicked laugh you know, a real contagious laugh. When you hear it you start laughing too, and before you know it everyone's at it!" Lon was smiling now as he remembered his dad. "I'd love to hear it again." Sophie thought she would change the conversation.

"You have a funny accent, where are you from?"

"Siren's Dunes of course! Me Mam and Dad were from Liverpool, suppose I sound like them."

"Your mum sounds nothing like a Liverpod. . . Liverpudlian!"

"She does really, she just puts on that Madam Izabela accent for the punters, you know."

"Oh I see." Sophie and Lon fell silent for a moment. "Lon, it's gone very quiet in the house. Do you suppose Jack's gone to bed?" Both Sophie and Lon fell silent and they strained their ears to listen for any sound that would tell them to stay put. They couldn't hear a thing.

"Okay Sophie, this is the plan. We open the door bit by bit, keep listening for Jack. If it's safe, we'll try to get out and go home." Sophie agreed. Turning the handle slowly, Sophie inched open the door.

Chapter 18
The crab was alive

The police had responded to Helen's emotional call for help and were round at gull cottage promptly. Two Police officers came initially, a man and a woman. They both interviewed Tom and Helen thoroughly and Tom took the male officer, PC Duggan, upstairs to see Sophie's bedroom. Officer Duggan carefully examined the room looking for clues as to where Sophie may have gone. He asked Tom if she had made any friends during the holiday but Tom explained that they had only been at Siren's Dunes a couple of days and Sophie had spent almost all of her time with them. Duggan picked up on what Tom had said.

"Has Sophie at any time been anywhere on her own?" Duggan asked.

"Erm. . . I think. . . yes! Yes she has. This morning she went out to spend her pocket money. Just the local shops, down the street you know."

"Did she say if she met anybody whilst she was out? Did she seem in a funny mood when she returned?"

"No. No she seemed fine, we went out together after that. She said nothing." Tom could hardly answer officer Duggan's questions; his head was in a spin with worry.

"We understand that you had a burglary the previous night. Perhaps this had affected your daughter."

"Oh god, you don't think she's been kidnapped do you? You don't think the burglar returned?" Tom was panic-struck.

"I don't think the two incidents are connected Mr Sealey, please try to calm down, we will need your help."

In the living room of the cottage Helen was searching through her purse. The other policewoman, officer Jackson, had asked Helen if she had a recent photograph of Sophie.

"Yes here it is, it's about a year old. But she hasn't changed really." Helen handed the picture to officer Jackson. It was one of those passport photographs you have taken in a booth. The officer noticed the prominent white streak in Sophie's hair, it would be easy to spot her with such a characteristic she thought.

"Do you have anything larger?" the officer asked.

"No, not here. It's the only picture I have with me. All our albums are at home in Cambridge."

"That's ok, we will be able to have this enlarged, it will do nicely." Tom and officer Duggan had rejoined the others in the living room. The photograph was handed to officer Duggan and he used his radio to contact the police station.

"Has Sophie ever done anything like this before?" officer Jackson enquired.

"Never. This is totally out of character for Sophie. I can't think why. . . " Helen sobbed. Officer Duggan asked Tom if he would like to accompany him whilst he took the patrol car around the town. Tom agreed. Helen was asked to remain at the cottage with officer Jackson in case Sophie returned.

Tom and officer Duggan proceeded along the main street. It was a dark night. Many of the street lamps were not working. The only light they had was the patrol car headlights; this made the search all the more difficult. Tom was anxious, he had the patrol car passenger window completely open and his head pushed out as far as it would go. He would call out for Sophie every time he saw a shuffling figure in the gloom.

"I'd like to pop into the station sir, to get this photograph copied. The other patrol cars could do with something to use to identify Sophie," explained officer Duggan. Tom said nothing. He was in a world of his own and was only vaguely listening to what the police officer was saying to him. "I'm sure we'll find her sir, I'm sure everything will be alright," continued officer Duggan. The patrol car turned into the police station.

......

Sophie and Lon inched along the hallway. The house was old and the floorboards, all warped and eaten away by generations of woodworm creaked and snapped under their feet. As they got nearer to the front room they became aware of loud snoring. Sophie was the first to poke her head around the door. She saw the back of a tatty old armchair, and a messy mop of white hairs that sprouted from Jack's head.

Sophie glanced at the supper table and saw the box of wines. She saw two empty green bottles

lying on the floor next to the armchair. Jack's hand dangled above them whilst he slept. Lon was next to peer into the room,
"He's sound asleep... I think," whispered Sophie.
"Drunk too, look at the empty bottles." Lon pushed past Sophie and entered the room.
"Lon, be careful!" Sophie was worried in case Jack was a light sleeper.
"Nah! He's wrecked." Lon had stopped whispering.
"Let's get out of here then, come on Lon." Sophie left the room and made her way to the front door. Lon noticed the golden claw poking out of its leathery sack.
"Hey Sophie come and see this!" shouted Lon. Jack stirred in his sleep and Lon froze. Jack's snoring soon resumed and Lon let out the breath he had been holding.
"Lon, what are you trying to do?" scolded Sophie still whispering.
"Sorry, I forgot. I saw this, you have to see." Sophie edged into the front room once more to see what Lon was looking so closely at. When she saw it she gasped.
"Beautiful," she said. "Where do think he got it from?" Sophie pondered.
"Probably stole it, knowing old Jack." Lon added. Sophie gently ran her fingertips across the jewels that were embedded into the crab's shining shell. Her fingertips came to rest upon the two ruby like gems that were the crab's eyes. Sophie pulled her hand off the golden crab. She had just

seen something that made her shout for joy. Jack waffled momentarily in his sleep, disturbed by Sophie's squeal.

"My sea ring Lon! Look there it is!" Just a few inches behind the crab lay the mermaid's ring. Sophie leaned forward and reached for the ring.

"Sophie look out!" cried Lon. Steam surged out from the golden crab's slit mouth. Sophie withdrew her hand. Both Sophie and Lon watched in amazement as the crab came alive. One by one its legs unfolded, and its huge pincer-claw sprung open revealing a razor sharp cutting edge. The crab's ruby-like eyes suddenly flashed on like two bright red bulbs. They swivelled on their stalks as if scanning the room. Sophie and Lon backed slowly away from the table. The golden crab was now looking straight at them.

Chapter 19
A cavern beneath the sea

Into the depths, deep below the turbulent ocean was a cave. The cave unbeknown and unseen by human eyes had existed for thousands if not millions of years. Fashioned by the elements and once inhabited by sea serpents and other long ago creatures.

Inside the wondrous cavern, where the walls sparkled and glittered like a trillion stars, were three large thrones. The middle throne being the largest of the three was laden with gold and silver and studded with bulbous gems and pearls. The two smaller thrones either side were equally richly decorated.

The thrones stood upon a rock island that was surrounded by a sea pool of brilliant blue rippling water. On the middle throne sat Melusa, the last surviving mermaid of Siren's Dunes, possibly the last mermaid in the whole world.

Melusa was watching the wall of the cavern in front of her. Over thousands of years, salt had been deposited on the rock wall, its crystal surface now hardened and changed by the passing of time. Some of the salt had formed a shiny indent, smooth, like a mirror. Melusa had upon her head a large crown. The crown was made partly from gold, and partly from the curious crystal material used to make the identity rings worn by all merfolk past and present. The crown allowed Melusa to control the golden crab in old Jack's house. She did this using only her thoughts. The salt mirror allowed Melusa to use the golden crab's eyes, to see what the crab could see.

The mirror revealed two children, a boy and a girl. They had terrified faces and were backing away. Melusa could see a table top, and as the crab moved about on the table top she could see that she was in a dwelling, a human dwelling. Then she saw him, Jack, the one who had her ring and used it to control her.

Jack was sleeping in his armchair, and she was pleased. The special wine she had given to him had contained a sleeping spell. But she didn't expect to find children in Jack's house. This she thought might disrupt her plan, but the mirror then revealed what she was hunting. Her ring was lying on the table unguarded. Melusa closed her eyes and concentrated. The crab had to do its job now and do it very well.

Sophie and Lon had backed almost out of the room completely. Jack was still snoring, oblivious to what was scuttling about noisily on his supper table. The golden crab used the smaller of its two claws to scoop up the ring.

"Lon look. It's got my ring!" shouted Sophie, no longer afraid of waking Jack. The golden crab raised the ring and brought it closer to its stalk eyes. "What's it doing?"

"I don't know but it seems to want the ring!" said Lon.

"We have to stop it. I want my ring back Lon!" Sophie's shouting had finally managed to rouse

Jack from his slumber. Jack sat forward in his armchair and rubbed his eyes. When he opened them, he saw Sophie and Lon rushing towards the table.

"Eh? Whassht goin' on? Who are ye?" Jack blurted, still sleepy and very much muddled.

"Jack's awake Lon!"

"Bloody hell run for it Sophie." Lon sprinted past Jack's chair but one of Jack's arms shot out incredibly fast for a man of his age and present condition catching Lon's pullover.

"Caught ye in my house did I, ye thieving little pirate." Jack was now on his feet.

"Lon! Oh my god!" Sophie stood stupefied in the middle of the room. Jack heard Sophie's wailing and turned to see her.

"Eh? Another pirate. Come 'ere ye little ragtag." Lon slipped out of his pullover and darted underneath the supper table. Jack flung the empty pullover onto the floor and gripped the edge of the table. Before Jack pushed the table onto its side, Sophie witnessed something odd. A small piece of the crab's shell flipped open and the crab tossed the Sea ring inside. The shell then closed shut.

Everything spilled onto the floor when the table was overturned, the box of wines shattered onto Jack's tatty carpet. The golden crab fell heavily next to Sophie's feet and she stepped back in surprise. Lon kicked Jack in the shin and then ran for the front door.

"Sophie quick, let's run for it!"

"Ah! Me leg, you little scamp. Just wait, I'll have ye for that!" Jack was angry and he cursed a lot. Lon fiddled with the front door and managed to get it open.

"Come on Sophie, move it!"

Sophie wasn't going anywhere without her Sea ring, not after all this trouble. The golden crab was lying on its back, it was having trouble trying to get back onto its feet. Sophie knew how to handle crabs, but she wasn't going to take any chances with this one. Sophie picked up Lon's discarded pullover and threw it over the golden crab. She then scooped it up off the floor, keeping it wrapped tightly in the pullover. Jack saw Sophie seize his golden treasure.

"Ere, what are ye doing? That be my property, get your thieving mitts off it, do ye hear me!" Sophie ran to Lon who was standing on the front door step.

"Let's go Lon, I've got the crab!"

"For god's sake Sophie leave it. It's totally mad and could be dangerous." Before Sophie could answer Lon, Jack came stumbling towards them both screaming with rage. Sophie ran out through the open doorway into Jack's front garden, Lon was close behind.

"Just wait. Just wait till I get me hands on ye!" Jack launched himself from his house. Sophie jumped through a gap in Jack's crumbling wall. Lon was not so lucky. He stumbled over an old pile of bricks hidden in Jacks wild lawn and fell. Jack caught up with him.

"Go Sophie, run!" Sophie wanted to help Lon but there was nothing she could do. Jack pulled Lon to his feet and shook him by the arms.

"See, I aint too old to catch ye am I?"

"Sophie held up the bundle of pullover that contained the golden crab.

"Look I have your crab, your gold. If you want it back, you will have to catch me!" Jack pushed Lon to the ground and turned his attention to Sophie.

"An' I will too, I aint too old to catch a little ragtag!" Sophie turned and started running down the street. Jack hobbled after her cursing.

"I'll get help Sophie, don't worry!" shouted Lon from Jack's garden, but Sophie couldn't hear Lon, all she could hear was Jack's heavy boots stamping the pavement as he came after her.

......

Tom sat patiently nursing a plastic cup of weak tea whilst officer Duggan prepared some copies of Sophie's photograph. Every time a telephone rang in the police station Tom would sit up straight and strain his ears in case the call had anything to do with Sophie's disappearance. The phones were ringing every other second and it was turning Tom into a nervous wreck. Duggan returned carrying a handful of colour photocopies. He showed one to Tom.

"This is the best we could do, it's not bad, quite clear really. I will just go and sort out the distribution of these photographs, shouldn't take long". Tom was left on his own again, and the phones continued to buzz and ring.

......

Sophie kept running. The golden crab was beginning to feel heavy and she could feel its legs scratching about within Lon's discarded jumper. Still she had to carry on, Jack was close behind and she could hear his heavy footfalls and his coughing as he tried to catch up. As Sophie passed the funfair she stopped for a moment to catch back her breath. As she rested she peered into the darkness behind her to see if she could see exactly where Jack was. She became aware of a lurching shadow quite a distance down the street. It was him. Instinctively she ducked down low behind a parked car. Sophie remained concealed whilst a police car crawled along the street. The police car continued up the street passing Jack, illuminating him in the car's headlights. Sophie had no idea that the car was on a mission to find her, or that it contained her dad. Sophie's own guilt at breaking into Jack's house that night prevented her from calling for assistance. Instead she decided to make her way home.

Chapter 20
The dark and deserted funfair

Melusa studied the salt mirror but it revealed nothing to her, only blackness. The last thing she had seen through the crab's eyes was the table top at Jack's house, and then nothing. Melusa guessed that the crab had become contained within something or perhaps that despicable human, Jack had broken her mechanical aid. Melusa concentrated hard; there was only one way to find out. The crown on her head began to shine brightly. Soon the precious stones adorning it burned like fire.

Sophie dropped Lon's pullover the moment it began to smoulder. Terrified, Sophie stood up and backed away from the woollen bundle that had now burst into flames. Jack saw the fire and it gave away Sophie's position. Sophie watched as the golden crab emerged from the incinerated clothing, its stalk eyes shone red as it scanned its surroundings. Sophie reached out to grab the crab but its shell was steaming and she withdrew her hand guessing rightly that the crab would be too hot to handle.

The golden crab scuttled through Sophie's feet and underneath a gap in the fence that enclosed the funfair.

"Rabbits!" cursed Sophie as she watched the crab scurry away from her.

"Oi ye little ragtag, give us back me gold, an' I won't 'hurt ye!" It was Jack and he was close.

Sophie scanned the fence to the funfair; there was a hole in the wire that was big enough for her to squeeze into, but not Jack. Sophie climbed through the hole just seconds before Jack's head poked through. "Ye can't hide from me in there. You have summit of mine, and I won't let ye have it," spat Jack.

Sophie looked around the dark and deserted funfair. Now she had broken into a second place, she was alone, and more terrified than ever. Jack had begun to bend back the wire to the hole, making it larger. Sophie ran deeper into the lifeless funfair.

......

Lon stood outside Gull Cottage, he had run all the way and was out of breath. He intended to alert Sophie's parents to the danger that they had got into but the surprise at seeing a police car parked outside the cottage made him stop for a moment. Lon realised instantly that Sophie's parents must have discovered she was not in her bed and had called for the police. Lon took a final deep breath, now he had to explain all this to the police. He would be in trouble, there would be no doubt. But he had to help Sophie. Lon knocked on the front door and waited nervously for it to be opened. It was Officer Jackson who stood in the doorway and she left Lon tongue-tied.

"Yes, can I help you?" asked Jackson.

"I-I. . . w-we. . ." stammered Lon.

"Who is it? Is it Sophie? Has she come home?" Helen was now rushing to the open door.

"No. . . it. . . I am Lon, Sophie's in trouble, you've got to help her!" Lon blurted.

"Sophie? How do you know Sophie? Where is she? Tell me for heaven's sake!" Helen pleaded.

"Sophie. . . we broke into old Mister Cheese's. . . erm I mean Jack Chenes house! He's the one who burgled you last night. Sophie wanted to get your stuff back. I was helping her, but Jack caught us. Sophie and me, we got separated. I came as fast as I could. I'm sorry, really sorry!"

"You had better come inside young man, and start at the beginning," said Jackson, Lon was taken inside.

......

Jack was almost into the funfair now, he had clumsily got his shirt caught on the wire hole and was tugging at it furiously. Sophie had carefully run from booth to ride to booth, keeping out of sight the best she could.

The funfair looked odd in the night. The rides were all covered over with thick tarpaulins and looked so different in contrast to the daytime with all the coloured lights and loud music. All the booths were closed and looked so flimsy now, old and scruffy. The whole placed needed a fresh coat of paint Sophie thought. The only recognisable trait that made Sophie aware that she was indeed within a funfair was the faint smell of hotdogs and candyfloss that still lingered.

Sophie held her breath. She became aware of a shuffling sound far behind her. She guessed it was Jack and tiptoed around the side of the booth she was leaning against. Sophie peeped her head around the booth. She could see Jack and he was going in the opposite direction. Good she thought, then she glanced at the front of the booth that concealed her. It was Izabela's fortune booth, Lon's mum's booth. Sophie thought about Lon and hoped that he was alright.

Officer Jackson was parking the patrol car outside Lon's house. The house was all dark. Lon knew his mum would be asleep and dreaded the fact that he would have to explain himself all over again. The police had been stern with him already, but his mum would go ballistic. Jackson had informed the police station regarding Lon's news and all officers were now out looking for Sophie with heightened effort. Already, a police car had been sent round to Jack's house. The local police knew what sort of a character he was, not altogether too dangerous, but a villain nevertheless and one who had been arrested many times for burglaries around Siren's Dunes over the years.

The police found Jack's front door open and they went inside. All they could see was a room in disarray, a heavy table had been knocked over and there appeared to have been some kind of skirmish inside. There was no sign of Sophie or Jack. One of the policemen discovered Jack's hoard of gold coins. They were taken away for examination.

......

Sophie waited by Izabela's booth until Jack was well out of sight. As she waited, she could hear another familiar sound. Sophie peered at the darkened funhouse to the right of her, the scuttling sound was coming from there. Then she saw it, the golden crab with its radiant eyes and jewelled body, making its way past the funhouse towards the ghost train. Sophie took a glance behind her making sure Jack was nowhere to be seen, and then she dashed over towards the ghost train.

"Rabbits!" cursed Sophie. She wasn't fast enough and the crab had slipped underneath the ghost train's front stage and into the dark tunnel behind. Sophie stood in front of the ghost train, she certainly wasn't afraid of such amusements during the daylight, but now in the darkness, all alone, the ghost train was a foreboding place.

A discarded paper bag was scraped across the tarmac floor by the wind and Sophie spun around expecting to be confronted by Jack. She saw the bag come to rest momentarily by the ticket booth belonging to the ghost train before being whisked off on a new journey to the far side of the funfair. Sophie suddenly felt exposed in front of the ghost train. It was the fear that Jack might see her that forced her to climb the steps up onto the stage. Sophie stared at the tunnel in front of her. The phantoms painted around the tunnel glowed eerily in the night, some of them had been painted with fluorescent and illuminous paints. Sophie knew they were only harmless drawings and she took a deep breath and entered the tunnel.

Chapter 21
Under the ring's spell

Izabela was angry at being woke up in the middle of the night. She had no idea that Lon was missing from his bed and immediately told him off. She went berserk when Jackson told her about what Lon and Sophie had been up to and that Sophie was now missing and possibly in great danger.

"How could you be so stupid!" Izabela shouted.

"Sorry Mam, I really am," said Lon almost in tears.

"Your son has been stupid, but he did the right thing going to Sophie's parents. Now at least we know what happened to her," officer Jackson added.

"It's so awful. How are her parents coping?" wondered Izabela not knowing how she would cope if Lon was missing.

"They are extremely worried. It's only to be expected. I should go back to them now Lon is safe at home."

"Please let us know as soon as there is any news," asked Izabela.

"Of course, anyway I will be back in the morning. This kind of escapade can't simply be forgotten." Officer Jackson gave Lon a serious stare. Lon looked at his mum's angry face and then at the floor feeling both ashamed and worried.

......

It was so black inside the ghost train. Sophie could barely see her hand in front of her when she held it out. This was definitely not a very good idea at all she thought, after something long and furry brushed past her face. Sophie tried to follow the tracks on which the train, when in operation, travelled upon. At times, she stumbled over them and at one point she fell onto something pointy and cold. Reaching into her pocket Sophie took out the small plastic torch she had been carrying. She switched it on.

The torch was still working but only produced a weak beam of light that began to diminish slowly. Sophie discovered what the cold pointy object was that she had fallen onto. It was an oversized ridiculous looking plastic skeleton. Sophie saw a faint red glow from further along the tunnel. Using her torch, she followed the light, this time treading more carefully so as to avoid another collision with any more plastic skeletons.

The failing beam from Sophie's torch picked out the image of a mermaid painted onto the doors near the end of the tunnel. She remembered the painting from the first time she had ridden the ghost train. It looked even more spooky now. She guided the torch light away from the painting which had given her the shivers and she used it to illuminate the area of tracks where she had last seen the red glow. Sophie was elated when her torch revealed the golden crab, it looked at her with its stalk eyes before scuttling sideways under the stationary ghost train. In her excitement at locating the crab Sophie failed to notice that Jack had been slowly creeping up on her. She was now within his grasp.

Melusa saw Sophie on the salt mirror. She wondered who this human girl was. Everywhere her crab went, this girl was also there. The mirror also revealed the painted mermaid behind Sophie. Melusa looked at the ugly representation of a mermaid. Is that how humans see us she wondered? Melusa could see some shadowy shape moving behind the girl. She stared hard at the salt mirror and her eyes began to shine. The mirror seemed to magnify the shadowy shape revealing it to be Jack Chenes, the human she disliked the most. Melusa watched as Jack gripped Sophie's shoulder turning her around to face him. Sophie got a terrible shock when she found herself staring into Jacks cruel features.

"Got ye! Now ye little ragtag, where's me gold eh?" Jack spat.

"I-I-I don't know, honest!"

"Ye little liar. Hand it over, an Jack will let ye go!"

"Please mister Cheese, I don't have your gold, I just want to go home," pleaded Sophie terrified.

"What did ye just call me? Mister Cheese?"

"I-I-I'm sorry I didn't mean to–"

"Ye think ye can make fun of me do ye? Well I'll show ye I will, I'll show all the brats in this town!" Jack roared. Jack then felt something heavy attached to his trouser leg. Looking down he saw the golden crab, but this discovery did not please Jack too much. The crab was climbing up Jacks leg using its pincers to grasp folds of Jack's skin on its ascent.

"Yiarrgh! Get im off, get im off, the little devil!" screamed Jack in pain.

Sophie watched Jack dancing about and shaking his leg. The crab was firmly attached to Jack and he tried to dislodge the golden crab with his hands but it only made things worse as the crab dug its pincers in deeper. Unable to stand the pain any more Jack began to hammer his fists onto the crab. The hammering took its toll on the crab snapping off its stalk eyes and its shell opened releasing the mermaid's ring that fell to the floor. Jack saw the ring fall out of the crab but before he could do anything, Sophie reached out and grabbed it.

"Ere, keep your thievin' mits off that! It's mine!" ordered Jack.

"It was mine, and you stole it!" answered Sophie bravely. Sophie slipped the ring onto her finger without thinking about the possible dangers of doing such a thing, she just didn't want to lose it again. Suddenly the ring began to flicker into life. Sophie's whole hand glowed. She could see the bones and veins beneath her skin; her own blood pumping around from wrist to fingertip and back to wrist. As she looked at the ring, she began to forget who she was. In no time at all Sophie was in a trance. With the golden crab still firmly attached to his trousers, Jack came at Sophie and made a grab for the ring. Sophie calmly withdrew her hand and Jack snatched only at thin air.

"I told you to. . . " Jack was silenced when he looked at Sophie's eyes. They were shining a fiery bright yellow. The last time Jack had seen anything like this was when he had been on the small outcrop of rocks at the beach talking to the mermaid. "Oh, your face. . .eyes have gone all queer like!" Jack spluttered. Sophie raised her hand and pointed a finger at Jack. The ring pulsed light as it sat on Sophie's finger and a beam of pure white light shot out from Sophie's hand and hit Jack square between the eyes. Jack groaned and fell to his knees, "my eyes, I can't see, you've blinded me!" Jack cried. Sophie slowly turned and walked towards the exit of the ghost train; she was still in her trance.

......

Melusa studied the salt mirror, it resembled more of a map now. The map was of Siren's Dunes and showed the town and coastal areas. A red pinprick of light flashed from an area on the map where the funfair stood. The red light was slowly moving away from the funfair and towards the shore. Melusa removed the crown from her head and placed it to rest upon one of the empty thrones standing next to her. It was time for her to make a journey. In one single movement, Melusa slid off the throne and plunged into the rippling waters that formed the floor of the cavern. With a thrust of her powerful fishtail, she was soon propelled deep into the almost fathomless blue sea.

Tom and Officer Duggan had parked the patrol car across the road from the funfair. It was during their eighteenth circuit around the town that Tom had seen a strange and brilliant flash of light from somewhere within the fair. They decided to investigate in case it had anything to do with Sophie's disappearance. It was Tom who noticed the hole in the fence that Jack had used to climb through. Duggan had noticed something else. On the pavement near to the kerb was a pile of ashes and bits of what looked like a red sweater. Duggan picked it up and showed it to Tom.

"Was Sophie wearing this? Duggan asked. Tom briefly looked at the remains of the sweater.

"No. She didn't have anything like that, as far as I know."

"All the same I think we better hang onto this, just in case. You seem interested in that fairground sir." Duggan noticed that Tom was scanning the amusement park intensely.

"Well like I said I thought I saw a light. We all came here yesterday, we had fun."

"I understand sir, but we should get back to the patrol car and carry on the search."

"Yes you are right come o–" Tom silenced himself; there came a crashing noise from within the fairground. "Did you hear that?"

"Yes I did sir, come on we'd better take a look." Dugan and Tom squeezed through the hole in the fence.

Inside the ghost train Jack had stumbled and knocked the plastic skeleton off its pedestal. Its limbs had been sent crashing to the ground and its large bone-like head had rolled down the tracks and out of sight. Jack rubbed his eyes again. His vision was starting to return. He was glad, fearing that he had been blinded. But, after all, it was just a temporary thing. Like when someone takes your photograph with a flash camera, all Jack could see was a huge great circle of light blotting out most of everything else. Jack's vision may have been momentarily lost, but his hearing was fine. Jack could hear voices, men's voices outside the ghost train. Jack listened carefully.

Chapter 22
Melusa

Sophie descended the corroded set of iron steps leading to the beach. She was still under the spell of the ring and almost looked as though she was sleepwalking as she trudged along the sand below. The wind was strong this close to the sea, but even the strength and coolness of the wind failed to wake Sophie from her charmed state. She walked on.

Sophie was heading towards the outcrop of jagged rocks that seemed to haphazardly sprawl out to greet the thrashing waves. The ring on her finger still pulsed and shone as she walked on the wet sand. The waves gently rolled into shore spilling over her feet and soaking them, but still Sophie couldn't be awakened. She walked on.

Standing at the jagged rocks, Sophie scanned them with her gleaming eyes; she was looking for the easiest way to get on top. Soon she discovered the simplest route and began to climb. The rocks were slimy and slippery with sea-moss but she managed to make it all the way to the top. Sophie walked to the furthest most tip of rock and stood still. She waited and she waited, not knowing why she was waiting, not even knowing that she was there at all. The sea spray soaked her from head to toe, the wind tried to steal away her flimsy clothing. Still she waited.

......

Izabela paced up and down on her living room carpet. Lon was in his pyjamas still feeling ashamed and ridden with guilt for getting Sophie into this awful mess. He had lost count of the number of times his mother had told him off since the police woman had left the house. He was too worried to sleep and Izabela allowed him to wait up with her for the news of Sophie's safe return had come.

Lon was sent to fetch Izabela's box of fortune cards that she kept in her bedroom. Whilst he was upstairs Izabela cleared away the clutter that had accumulated on their dining table during the night, mostly coffee cups and the remains of various late night and early morning snacks. It was hungry business all this waiting. Lon returned with the box.

"Is this it Mam?" Lon handed Izabela a carved wooden box.

"Yes love, now I need you to be very quiet so I can concentrate."

"No worries Mam." Izabela sat at the table and took a set of fortune cards out of the wooden box. Lon watched his mum as she carefully shuffled the deck of cards. One by one Izabela placed down a card on the table and concentrated on it for a moment or two before placing another on top of it. Lon had seen his mum use this particular set of fortune cards before. They weren't the cards she used whilst at work in her booth at the fairground, these were her special cards that she claimed always tell her the important news she needed.

The cards looked very old each was frayed around its edge but they contained the most beautiful and vivid pictures that Lon had ever seen. Izabela had placed nine cards down onto the table already and each time she would shake her head and then select the next card from the top of the deck. Izabela selected the final card and immediately she became exited.

"Yes, I know where she is! Quickly Lon bring me the telephone!" she shouted urgently. Lon collected the walk-about phone from off its stand in the kitchen and handed it to his mother. She quickly dialled the number of the local police station.

"Yes my name is Izabela, I am calling about the missing girl Sophie Sealey, I know where she is!" Lon walked over to the dining table and looked at the final card that had been placed faced up in the centre. The card had a picture of a woman standing on a rock, completely surrounded by water. "Go to the beach, she is at the beach. Be quick. She is in danger!" Izabela said.

......

Sophie was drenched, but still unaware of where she was, she simply stared out to sea with the most luminous eyes. Somewhere far out at sea a sound began to be rolled in shore, carried on the back of the waves; pushed by the wind. It was singing, beautiful singing that could be heard, and it began to wake Sophie from her trance. Jack hid crouching low in the carriage of the ghost train. Tom and Duggan were having a look around. All the time they were talking about

Sophie. Jack guessed that Sophie was the girl who had gone off with his ring, the little ragtag who had broken into his home with that gypsy boy. Dugan moved closer to Jack's carriage and Jack held his breath.

"Hey look at this!" Tom called to Duggan.

"What is it? Found something?" Duggan walked back over to Tom and Jack let out his breath.

"Not sure what it is." Tom handed one of the golden crab's eyes to Duggan.

"Is this something of Sophie's?" Duggan asked as he examined the eye.

"I don't think so, but it looks valuable, is it gold?" Before Duggan could reply his radio buzzed into life calling for him to answer. It was the police station, they said that they had reason to believe Sophie was at the beach. As soon as Tom heard this he rushed out of the ghost train. Duggan ran after him. Jack also heard the radio and his years of working at the fair had taught him a quicker way to get down onto the beach. He thought if that girl was at the beach she must be using the ring to call to his mermaid. Only Jack knew exactly where Sophie would be.

Cold, wet and shivering, Sophie woke up to find herself stood precariously on a knobbly bit of rock; her feet were frozen solid as were her arms and face. The sudden awakening to the pain of her chills made her gasp, "m-m-my g-g-god, w-w-where am I-I?" she spoke through chattering teeth. The only warm part of her whole body was her right hand. She looked at it. It was still glowing slightly, and the mermaid's ring flashed and sparkled almost as if signalling to something. Then she saw it. Far out at sea, swimming towards the rocks, was a thing.

At first she thought it was a seal, but then she saw its face. It was a woman, with long hair, and eyes that shone, swimming towards her. The singing got louder too. Sophie managed to get her frozen legs to move her away from the tip of the rock just in time. The woman in the water was close enough to touch the rocks now and when she did, for a moment, the whole rock seemed to sparkle.

"Girl of the land, you have something of mine that belongs on my hand," sang the woman.

"W-w-w-wicked! A m-m-m-m-mermaid, a r-real mermaid!" gasped Sophie in awe. The mermaid's eyes widened, and she smiled a wide smile revealing a set of pearly white teeth.

"Human child, you know of my race? Come closer to me, let me look at your face."

"N-n-no! I-I'm afraid t-to!"

"Please, there's no need to be afraid of me. I will not harm you, I cannot leave the sea." Sophie crouched low nearer to the water. The mermaid nodded, she recognised her as the girl who had been shown on the salt mirror throughout the night. "Melusa is my name, for you I came."

"I am Sophie, Sophie Sealey, I-I have your ring, it has your name on it!"

"Return to me my identity ring. It was given to me by a great sea king."

"I found it on the beach, and a man stole it from me. Why did he want this ring so badly, Mr Cheese I mean?" Sophie asked Melusa.

"When the ring is in someone else's hand, I have to obey their every command."

"I see. I suppose he made you get all those gold coins for him also."

"That man was greedy and used me as his slave, he desired all the treasure that is kept in my cave. To think that man was so easily beguiled, by nothing more than such a child."

"If the ring is so important to you, how come you managed to lose it?"

"It was many years ago, I became entangled in a fishing net, the ring slipped off my finger, I was careless I know. The sea king was angry that I had lost it that way, he ordered me to find it, I have tried till this day. Now I see it before my eyes, in the hands of someone so young yet so wise."

Sophie and Melusa talked and talked. Melusa told Sophie about her home beneath the sea and how she sometimes gets lonely being the last of the Merfolk. Sophie told Melusa that she had come to Siren's Dunes for a holiday and she told her that she understood what it was like to be lonely. Even though she had her mum and dad and loved them a whole bunch, she still missed Kooler her dog who died. She explained to Melusa how Kooler had been her best friend. Melusa listened to Sophie, she was fascinated by the stories that this land child told.

Sophie was growing colder by the minute, and she held out the ring for Melusa to take. Melusa swam nearer to Sophie and her eyes beamed when she looked upon her ring. Melusa took the ring from Sophie.

"You have returned my ring to me, I shall now place it somewhere safe, in my cave beneath the sea. I say this now, and do not pretend, you truly are my very good friend."

Melusa waved and Sophie watched her disappear beneath the waves. A faint glow lingered for a fleeting second, and then even that had gone. Sophie turned into the wind; it whipped her hair about her face as she climbed off the rocks down to the sand. The waves were crashing hard against the rocks and the noise they made masked the sound of Jack Chenes as he jogged across the sand towards Sophie. Sophie brushed her hair out of her eyes and saw Jack coming for her.

"You can't run away from me this time! Jack's got ye now ye little thief!" Jack roared as he grabbed Sophie's arm. Jack was right, Sophie couldn't run; she was too tired and the wind had frozen her legs. She looked at Jack's face, he seemed very old to her now. His white hair, what was left of it was flapping about his ears. His teeth were all rotten and stained by wine, and many were missing. But it was his eyes that worried her, they were staring at her crazily. "Now just tell old Jack where me ring is or I'll feed ye to the fish I will!"

Chapter 23
A new ring

Sophie closed her eyes; the cold was almost too much to bear. She wished that she was in her room all tucked up in bed reading her book about the boy wizard and his adventures and not having an adventure of her own. Sophie felt Jack's grip slip away and she opened her eyes to see him hitting the ground hard. Sophie almost wept with tears of relief when she saw her dad standing over him. Tom dragged Jack to his feet.

"Nobody lays a finger on my Sophie do you hear me!" Tom screamed at Jack. Jack's lip was bleeding.

"A-alright, let us go, I aint doing no harm mate honest," Jack blurted. Tom was about to hit Jack again when Officer Duggan caught up with Tom and Sophie.

"Please, don't do anything stupid sir, he's mine now. Let me take him." Tom pushed Jack towards Duggan who gripped him roughly. Sophie hugged her dad and they both stood there whilst the wind rocked them.

"Dad I'm sorry, so sorry."

"It's okay. All that matters is you're safe."

"Can we go home?"

"You bet!"

Jack was frog marched to a waiting police car by Duggan where two other police officers took over and handcuffed Jack before pushing him into the back of the car.

"She broke into my house she did, the little ragtag! Arrest her, go on, I aint done nothing wrong, I'm an old man!" squawked Jack.

"He's a thief! He stole my mum's jewellery and I can prove it!" shouted Sophie.

"Leave it for now love, let's go home, your mum is worried sick," Tom said before they climbed into Duggan's car.

"Dad, what about Lon is he. . . ?"

"Lon's fine. He came to the house, to get help."

"Thank god!" In no time at all Sophie was running up the path of Gull cottage straight into her mother's arms.

......

The following morning saw the return of Officer Jackson to Gull Cottage. Sophie, Tom, and Helen braced themselves for the worst, after all, breaking into even a burglar's home was a serious misdemeanour as far as the law is concerned.

Everyone was pleasantly surprised when Sophie was told that the police would not be taking the matter any further. Jackson told Sophie that they thought she had suffered enough from the whole affair, and Jack Chenes had himself decided not to press for charges against Sophie and Lon. Jack had been detained by the police on charges of burglary and Jackson had returned the stolen jewellery box much to Helen's delight. Officer Jackson also mentioned that they had found a huge hoard of old gold coins that Jack had claimed had been given to him; they were treating the find as suspicious. Sophie knew exactly where he had obtained the gold, the last living mermaid of Siren's Dunes had brought it to him.

Sophie had gone up to her room once officer Jackson had left the cottage, and she had spent an hour playing with her games console. When she had eventually got bored of her game she had returned to the living room only to discover Tom and Helen packing lots of their things into two big suitcases.

"Mum, what's going on? Where are we going?" Sophie asked puzzled.

"Your dad and I have decided that it would be best if we went home. The holiday hasn't turned out quite how we would have liked has it?"

"But it's only been a couple of days! We were supposed to go home at the weekend," said Sophie saddened by this sudden change to their holiday plans.

"Yes love, but we thought that you would have had enough of this place, after everything that's happened."

"I don't want to go home, not yet. I like it here really I do!" Sophie wanted to stay for a while longer. She did have a terrifying night at Jack's house and on the beach, but she had had a fantastical encounter with a magical mermaid, and also she had made a friend in Lon. She didn't want to just disappear without so much as a goodbye, and she did have such a lot to tell Lon about the mermaid. "Please Mum, just a couple of days that's all." Tom looked at Sophie. He couldn't believe that she wanted to stay at this town any longer. But they did come here to cheer her up in the first place; she seemed really happy to stay.

"Why don't you put the kettle on love, your mum and I will have a little chat about it." Tom said, and Sophie went into the kitchen obediently. After a nice cup of tea and a plate of custard creams, Tom announced that they would all spend another couple of days at the cottage much to Sophie's delight and they all went out for a burger followed by a walk on the beach.

......

The sun was shining and the cold wind that had prevailed the last day or so had finally gone. Sophie left Tom and Helen dawdling along the sand and she ran over to the outcrop of rocks that only the night before had served as an island whilst she talked with Melusa.

The rocks didn't seem so scary in the daylight, and Sophie climbed up on top. She walked to the further most tip of the rocks; the sea had all gone out at this time, and the rocks were only surrounded by a sheet of glittering sun-bleached sand. Sophie wondered what Melusa would be doing now and she tried to imagine what her home would be like beneath the ocean.

"Be careful love! You might slip and hurt yourself," came Helens cry from somewhere far behind the rocks. Tom shielded his eyes from the blinding sun using his hand. He could not believe Sophie was back at those rocks, where he had found her the previous night, cold and scared. He imagined it was a bit like when you fall off a bike or a horse, the best thing to do is get straight back on, to overcome the fear of falling off again. It usually does the trick, and he imagined that Sophie knew this and that was why she had asked to go back onto the beach and was now back at those rocks. Sophie of course wanted to see the beach and the rocks for totally different reasons to what her dad believed. It was on this beach, on these rocks that Sophie had talked with Melusa, and that was something you don't do every day. Sophie hoped that there would be a little piece of magic still remaining at the island of rocks, and Sophie was right.

Tucked away in a recess near the tip of the rock where Sophie stood something sparkled at her. Sophie immediately scooped whatever it was out of the hole and looked upon it with amazement. It was a beautiful shell made of a silvery material. It looked magnificent as it scattered sunbeams in every direction sitting on Sophie's hand. She saw that there was yet another treasure tucked inside the shell itself. Sophie tipped the shell and out fell a cool, green sea ring, not unlike the one she had herself returned to Melusa. At first she thought it was Melusa's ring but when she examined it, she saw that this ring had her name engraved onto it.

"A ring for me! A present from Melusa!" Sophie gasped with joy. The ring fitted perfectly on her middle finger, and as she slid it on, the sparkling shell let off a singing noise. Sophie pressed the shell to her ear, the singing continued,

'Thank you, thank you,' the melodic voice seemed to be saying over and over.

"Come on love, best get down from there," Tom shouted. Both he and Helen were now at the rocks. Sophie jumped down.

"Good heavens, what have you found?" Helen asked as she studied the shell in Sophie's hands.

"Oh, just a lovely shell, suppose the sea washed it in," said Sophie. As they all left the beach to make their way home, Sophie turned back to the outcrop of rocks. "Thanks Melusa." Sophie whispered.

......

That night was to be the last night at the cottage. They would be returning to their home in Cambridge the following day at about midday. Sophie was looking out of her bedroom window. It was so dark outside apart from the odd street lamp, she could hardly believe that she had climbed down from her window in the middle of the night and sneaked off to Jack's house. The sea ring on her finger and the shell on the windowsill told her that she had.

Sophie watched a man walking his dog outside. He passed underneath the street lamp and was bathed in its orange glow for a few seconds whilst he waited for his dog to finish off doing what every dog does at a lamppost, it made Sophie think about Kooler and how she still missed him.

Sophie's curtains were drawn now, lying in bed, Sophie was examining the silvery shell once more. Rolling it over in her hands she pressed the shell to her ear to see if she could hear the singing again. What she did hear made her heart leap with joy. The singing had been replaced with a barking, and Sophie recognised it as Kooler's barking. The shell was truly magical. whatever Sophie thought of, the shell would play to her the sounds associated with that thought. Sophie tried all sorts of things. She thought about her favourite songs, her family, and even her friend Lon. She could hear Lon talking and laughing just as they had both laughed when they had run from Jack's house the afternoon before their night of adventure. It was then Sophie realised what she had to do.

Chapter 24
Lemonade and biscuits

Sophie stood outside of Lon's house. She rang the doorbell. It had been difficult persuading her mum and dad to let her visit Lon again but it was their last day at siren's Dunes and Sophie was under strict orders to return by noon. When Izabela opened the door she greeted Sophie warmly and invited her inside. Lon was pleased to see Sophie and they began to exchange stories about police questions and what they both knew about Jack being locked up. Lon told Sophie that it was his mother Izabela who told the police where she was that night.

"She used her fortune cards, she knew exactly where you were," Lon said exited.

"Thanks Izabela, I don't know what I would have done if my dad and the police didn't find me when they did."

"You're very welcome Sophie, I am just glad I was able to help even if it was my son who got you into all this mess." Izabela glanced at Lon but Lon was too happy to be able to wipe the smirk off his face. Izabela went to fetch some lemonade and biscuits from the kitchen and Sophie used the time to tell Lon about Melusa.

"Lon I saw the mermaid!"

"You didn't!"

"I did Lon, and she was amazing! We talked, and I gave her back the sea ring. Apparently, Jack had been using it to control her, making her bring him gold, the coins and stuff we found in his house."

"What did she look like Sophie?"

"She was beautiful Lon. She had the loveliest eyes I have ever seen, and her skin was all sparkly. But, it was her voice I shall always remember. Whenever she spoke, it was like she was singing a lovely song. I wish you had been there Lon, to see Melusa!"

"So do I, but I had to get help when I saw old mister Cheese running after you!"

"I know, and I am grateful." Sophie took a glass of lemonade from Izabela and waited until she had left the room again before she showed Lon the sea ring that had her name on.

"K-e-w-l! How did you get that?" asked Lon puzzled.

"Melusa was grateful that I had returned her ring, she left me this one as a gift, look it has my name on it!"

"You are lucky Sophie," said Lon, slightly envious of Sophie's trinket.

"You helped too Lon, and there is something for you also." Sophie took the shell out of her coat pocket and handed it to Lon. "This shell's magic. You can hear anything you want in it, anything at all. It's yours. Just put it to your ear, you'll find out what it can do."

"Wow! Thanks Sophie, it's the best thing ever!" shouted Lon in excitement. "Better than my scrap book!"

Sophie left Lon's house exactly twenty minutes to twelve. They said their farewells and promised to email or text each other. Soon she was back at the cottage and they were all packed ready for their journey home.

The drive back to Cambridge was a sad one for Sophie, she had grown to love it at Siren's Dunes in the short time she had been there. Tom and Helen promised Sophie that they would return for many shorter breaks, but next time they would spend it in a more secure hotel.

......

One week after leaving Siren's Dunes Sophie received her first email from Lon. He told Sophie how he had spent many a day sitting on the small outcrop of rocks, looking out to sea, and hoping to catch a glimpse of the one and only lady of the sea. He also wrote about how the shell had replaced his personal music player. He said it was way better because it didn't need batteries. Lon said that he could now hear his dad's laugh again. Sophie was pleased.

Printed in Great Britain
by Amazon